# STORIES THAT WORDS TOLD ME

# EDWARD L. ALBAN

# STORIES THAT WORDS TOLD ME

# CONTENTS

# DEDICATION

---

*To JoAnn, Elizabeth, Thomas and Brian*

# FOREWORD

---

Spelling, intonation and definition are but the outward signs of words. Then there is the private inner core of the word, the personal component which encapsulates our memory of events, of people, of places which we associate with a word. This has to do with the how, the where and when a word entered our vocabulary. It is this personal dimension of words that inspired the poems, essays, memoirs and fictional narratives that follow. They are the little bonfires in my life that words lit.

At times, words are like children. They play impish games. They refuse to help a poet with rhyme. The first chapter captures this give-and-take with words. It happens that I was trying to compose, of all things, an ode to words. But words refused to co-operate with rhyme.

At other times, especially when traveling, foreign words enter our minds with such a splash that they etch themselves indelibly into our memory. How could I forget the Italian words *guasto* and *pazzia?* Each, in their own way, made their unforgettable entrance into my mind as recounted in the stories *Facial Words* and *Waif Words.*

Some words are at war with themselves. They embody two meanings which contradict each other. They are bizarre, museum pieces. They are so rare that you can't recall ever having used them. They emit no personal latent waves, no resonance from within. You just can't find an imprint of their footsteps in your life. They are just linguistic oddities. This was the case with so-called *Janus words,* words with two opposite meanings. Ultimately, I was able to find a word that touched my life, not in English but in Spanish. It was so weird that it deserved a story.

Some words are ephemeral. They bloom and die within a day as it were. This is the case with fashion words that surf on the fickle waves of fads, such as: ruff, stomacher, tabard, knickerbockers and farthingale. Words that Shakespeare used are examples. Some are long dead now. The chapter *Requiem for Lost Words* is a personal essay about such words.

And words, like people, have their own destiny. Some are healthy and vibrant; some are poor and sickly. If words could talk and tell us their stories, what would they say? In *Words Also Die,* I met a class of words who suffered a dismal dystopian fate.

Some words are intrinsically beautiful and carry in their aura a warm angelic kindness, like the word "smile," which I picture as having wings. Poets write songs about these words. Another such is "mama." This is especially poignant when it is the Mama who is desperately trying to hear that word from her baby. For this mama the enunciation of that word from her baby was an affirmation no less, a proclamation to the world that her baby would not be, as some feared, deaf, mute and blind. *First Word* deals with this and is based on a true story.

Of course, I am not the only one who has this inner sense for the extra dimension of words. Some people feel certain words vividly because for them a particular word carries a harm that dwells in the tissue of their scars. The word haunts them with an inexpugnable pang of guilt, regret, or sorrow. Just imagine the resonance of the word "rope" at the hangman's home. Racial words are another example. So sensitized is the soul of some people that they feel umbrage at the slightest hint of a word that sounds pejorative to them. The word "niggard," for example, has this radioactivity with Black people. It is a perfectly innocuous verb, but it has jagged edges for some Blacks.

Exotic weather words are so strange, and awkward that they inspire limericks. What else could one do with tsunami and haboob?

> *Haboob* and *tsunami* are so rare
> That they just don't scare.
> But not in Yemen, where only a boob
> Would go outdoors to see a Haboob.

> And in Fiji, people bolt from their *tatami*
> When the siren says *tsunami*
> Except for drunken fools who will stay put
> Because they just don't give a hoot.

And some words have vaudeville in their blood. They make cameo appearances and lend themselves to skits, puns, tongue twisters, faux amis, malapropisms, mondegreens, double-entendres, misunderstandings and pratfalls.

On another extreme, rhetorical words from ancient Greece –words such as anaphora, anadiplosis, metonymy, synecdoche, antonomasia and zeugma—have a lofty mien and codify the primeval tools of poetry. In the chapter *Word Fair,* two of these words come alive in the form of two women. They speak in their own distinctive manner, making a case for themselves. I don't need to add a word to clarify them. I just step back and leave the floor to them. Just listen to them, and you'll know what they mean.

I exult in the power of words to educate us and make us wiser, to take us to faraway places as our cicerones, our gondoliers, or sherpas. Words can be magic flying carpets. Imagine traveling on the wings of words all over the world without ever leaving your reading chair at home.

# WORDS, THE IMPS

I was trying to honor words with an ode. I begged for help with rhyme. But they refused. So, I left the ode without rhyme but took them to task with this rebuke:

> In dictionaries words appear from A to Z
> All in formation, eager aides to be
> Giving the impression they are dutiful slaves,
> While in my mind they're arrant knaves.
> They are anything but subservient
> They're wayward, disobedient.
>
> They don't come when they are called.
> They play games. They hide and stall,
> They malinger and refuse to help
> They're ornery little whelps!
>
> But then at other times the opposite is true.
> They flirt with writers, and they coo,

Especially when they want a role to play
They volunteer for duty at no pay.
They would be in a poem at all costs
They would star and be the host!

### My Ode to Words

Words ... scribbles lining paragraphs
Like seedlings in the furrows of a field
And blooming into gardens
In the expanses of the soul.

Words ... phonemes and morphemes
That flow in cadences and rhymes
To resonate within the heart
And titillate the intellect.

Words ... inchoate tiles in a linguistic mosaic
Holding their own upon a page
And waiting for the reader's mind
To unfold the mural's scape.

Words... filigrees of language
Golden gems adorning
Silver pendants holding
The garments of a thought.

Words ... doves in flight
Aflutter in verses
Carrying utterances of the heart
On their wings.

I pleaded for rhyme in the stanzas above!
I begged. But words are so capricious at times.

They just refused me and said: not today, Love.
So, I left the verses as you see them—without rhymes.

# FACIAL WORDS

We were at the Newark airport, waiting to board an Alitalia flight to Rome and the thrill of my Italian adventure had already begun. I could hear Italian words floating in the air and I would reach for them excitedly as if they were balloons or colorful iridescent soap bubbles. When I could catch their meaning, I would soar aloft with pride and the exultation would carry me on updrafts of understanding. But, more often, when the bubble would soar too high, I would just catch the spray as it popped and vanished, leaving me blank.

The flight was already running two hours late and they announced the reason over the intercom, saying in Italian that it was due to un guasto al motore. I got the motor part. But, un guasto? I missed that bubble.

Fortunately, sitting nearby was an Italian family. The husband, who had been reading a magazine, had missed part of the announcement and asked his wife about it. She repeated it: "Un guasto al motore." She articulated it in such a theatrical unmistakable way that I couldn't help catching the meaning from her malleable face whose contorted moues spoke volumes. Her face reminded me of those still pictures of a boxer being pummeled in the ring, each frame showing the effect of a blow; the lips twisting; the eyes wincing; the cheeks cringing as if they were made of play dough. I've seen such disappointment before when a vending machine gulps your money and gives you nothing; when a pen goes dry just when you needed to write something desperately. From the grimaces of this expressive woman, I deduced that guasto had to be a breakdown. So, I learned my first Italian word for the trip not from a book, or dictionary, but from a face, a morphing lexicographic Italian face contorting as if defining the word in pantomime. Bravo, bravo signora! I shall never forget *guasto*.

# WAIF WORDS

Usually, a word enters our minds through deliberate actions on our part. We look it up in dictionaries; we consult its etymology or spelling. We work to make it our own. It is only after much deliberate effort that we can usher it into our family of words.

But sometimes, it is the word that chooses us. A word knocks at our senses again and again; it bumps into us through independent chance encounters whose recurrence seems, in retrospect, more like persistence than repeated happenstance. Like a ubiquitous waif, the word follows you around. It catches your eye. You ignore it at first, you move on and you even forget about it for a time. But it persists. It catches your ear. You turn a corner, and you find it on a billboard. You travel across town on a train, only to find the word just outside the station when you disembark. You find it in a magazine, on the TV; you hear it on the radio; you overhear it from the lips of strangers. Until finally, at some point, the doorman of your mind finally asks: "Little word lost, do you want a home?"

So it was that I learned the Italian word pazzia. We had been in Rome for three days and were walking to the Museum of Modern Art in the Villa Borghese. It was a rainy day in December 1995. I looked around me with the voraciousness of a tourist, rubbernecking, gaping. What do they do for Christmas in this most Catholic of world capitals? What sort of movies are playing now?

The rain would intensify sporadically, forcing us to crowd into store entrances, to scurry from news kiosk to trinket stall in search of shelter. Suddenly, out of nowhere, battalions of Indian vendors appeared in the streets selling umbrellas. It was as if they had been sitting on truckloads of umbrellas in Bombay or Bangladesh, praying fervently for rain, and Rome had been the first city to come up with a demand for their supply. They came at us rushing and we bought their umbrellas.

Such were the surprises of Rome on this rainy morning. While I did not expect to find the Christmas hoopla and frenzied commercialism of U.S. cities, I did expect to see at least a crèche now and then and I did expect to hear the polyphonic strains of ancient canticles, the sweet and lofty choruses of boy sopranos singing Ave Marias. Incredibly, the Christmas motif was virtually nonexistent in full mid-December. Nor, come to think of it, I did not expect to find umbrella peddlers from India. Neapolitan tenors yes, or perhaps also, Venetian falsettos crooning their wares. And where was Fellini? Marcello? Sofia? I could not find them. Instead, I found English spoken movies. By chance we passed by a theater where they were playing "The Madness of King George," a movie we had seen in the U.S. a few weeks before.

The rain had completely stopped by the time we reached the old city wall. We entered the Villa Borghese and made our way to the museum under a shining sun that turned this rainy wintry day into a splendid spring-like day. The art exhibit was especially refreshing after seeing so much Renaissance and religious art in the Vatican and the Sistine Chapel the previous days. It was a welcome change to see Klees, Chiricos, and an entire section of early Mondrian.

One large oil painting made an indelible impression. It featured a disheveled woman who was walking out of a room in such a state of despair that she seemed to be escaping not only from the room in the painting, but from the canvas, from her skin, from her body and from this world. Who the artist was, I can't recall. But I shall never forget the title of the painting: "Pazzia."

There was a word that none in our group knew. We conjectured it could mean 'madness' because the woman had a freaked-out look, as if she were standing on a high voltage line, or as if she had seen evil incarnate. Her hair radiated from her gaunt head as though each thread had been shot straight out of her scalp like a serpentine. Her face had a grimace of anguish. One could almost hear her shrieking.

We moved on to happier paintings and shortly thereafter to the cool, fresh air of the streets of Rome on a beautiful day. Our walk took us by the theater where we had seen the poster of the movie "The Madness of King George." But this time I was close enough to read its Italian title. And there I saw that word again. The Italian title was: La Pazzia di Re Giorgio. I yanked my wife by the arm and pointed out the title to her. Her face beamed immediately with understanding as she also connected with the crazed woman in the painting. That clinched it for us. Pazzia meant "madness."

Over the next two days I would see or hear this word at least two more times. That evening watching television, I tuned into a talk show that seemed quite lively, full of antics and wild goings on. The host commented as he settled down to announce a commercial: "Ah, quelle pazzia." When we packed our bags to leave Rome two days later, I put away the maps, tour books, souvenirs, and, of course, the umbrellas. The word pazzia was among the souvenirs. But it was not a waif word anymore. It had found a home with me.

# JANUS WORDS

---

J anus words are rare and problematic. They typically have two meanings which contradict each other. Their name derives from Janus, the god from Greco-Roman mythology who had two faces—one which looked ahead and the other, in the back of his head, which faced the world behind him.

The word *cleave* is an example; it means to cut asunder, but it can also mean to merge together. So, you can cleave together what you first cleaved apart. The word *strike* is another example. It has Janus-like properties because to strike a ball means to hit it, but in baseball, if you swing at the ball and don't hit it, that is also called a strike. Finally, the word *inflammable* is a Janus word because its synonym is *flammable*. Normally, the prefix *in* negates the meaning of a word. But in this case, inflammable remains flammable. To negate it you would have to use another prefix and say: nonflammable.

It's a good thing that Janus words are rare, otherwise their mischief would be too chaotic to be funny. Language would be too entangled to be useful. This was one instance when I came up blank, without any personal resonance from a Janus word. I could name nothing more than *cleave* and *flammable* and neither one invoked personal memory. But something in me kept insisting I was wrong; yes, there was a Janus word pulsing inside me. I just happened to be looking in the wrong language. I found it eventually—not in English, but in Spanish. That Janus word was *Ordenador* and it caused so much mischief and confusion that it deserved a story. On the one hand it refers to someone who gives orders; but, also to someone who takes orders.

My experience with this word goes back to the late 80s. I first heard it in the Spanish song, *Mi Ordenador*, sung by the popular Spanish diva Paloma San Basilio. The song had a sweet beautiful, plaintive melody which I liked. But the lyrics turned me off and I deliberately ignored them. I had formed the impression that it was about a young woman who was in love with her boss, an abusive order master (ordenador) who bossed her around and I didn't want to know the details. I resented the abusive situation. How could she love a bossy tyrant? And how could they waste such a beautiful melody in such a situation?

Then one day, I came to a part in the song that completely baffled me. It forced me to pay attention to the lyrics. The young woman said: "yesterday my order master committed suicide."

What? How is this? Did the tyrant commit suicide? This doesn't make sense. Why would he? This is so out of character. I could see her killing herself. Much as she loved him, she had enough abuse, but why would he kill himself? No way! The song bugged me, and I made up my mind to hear it through and through until it made sense, once and for all.

And so, I did. That same day, back in the 80s, I got to the bottom of it and discovered that the word *ordenador* in Spain did not stand for an order-giver, but for an order-taker. In fact, to

Spaniards an *ordenador* was just a PC, a personal computer. PCs were just coming out in those days. Their names were still in flux. They called them one thing in the Americas and something else in Spain. In the rest of the Spanish-speaking world, including here in the U.S., a PC is called a *computadora,* which is close to the English word "computer."

But why did they call them that in Europe? The French, by the way, also call a PC an *ordinateur.* The reason is that the Europeans were focused on the order-taking property of a computer. After all, a PC is an electronic factotum that takes your orders and delivers results.

The upshot of this is that I had the song all wrong. The song was not about the young woman loving her order-master despite his tyranny. Rather, it was about the order-taker, the computer, falling in love with its owner, the young woman.

She lived alone and the PC was her sole companion, her robotic roommate. The song tells of the time when she first noticed the PC acting strangely. He began to act as if he were a man in love. He stared at her. At times she felt denuded and embarrassed to the point she had to put a cover over him and turn him off. He got progressively worse. He did all the things that—according to her—men in love supposedly do. He lied; he flirted; he talked silly; he giggled; he messed up on the job and he showed signs of jealousy. When she asked him to explain himself, he would just say: "love, love, love." Then, one day, suddenly, her PC blew a circuit and died. His screen turned off for good and he became forever silent. In her heart she knew there was more to it. He hadn't just blown a fuse. She felt sure he had committed suicide, and she was very, very sad. This was the true gist of the song.

The new sense of the word changed the dynamics of the situation completely and gave me a new parallax for the characters in the song. The order-meister went from being a tyrant to being a subservient go-fer, while the suppressed helpless young woman morphed from being a maid, to being the boss of the castle. She, it turned out, was the real temptress, the unreachable star.

I came to like the song all the more in its corrected sense because it played on the theme of futile impossible love, and it reminded me of another hapless lover from another age. I recalled a story by Theophile Gautier entitled *One of Cleopatra's Nights*, where a young slave fell in love with his beautiful and ruthless queen, Cleopatra. Unable to find any hope for his impossible love, he did what his heart told him to do, and he, too, committed suicide by daring to give his love free rein. Late one night he managed to make his way through the long labyrinths of the palace, and he sneaked past the eunuch guards and managed to get all the way into Cleopatra's chamber itself. There he surprised the empress and told her:

"I know I am as good as dead. So, kill me. But first be mine."

# REQUIEM FOR DEAD WORDS

The attic of the grand old house was huge. It covered the length and width of the house below and it contained a treasure of relics, discarded artifacts, furniture, toys, clothing, books, newspapers and magazines accumulated over 85 years. There were military uniforms and memorabilia from World War II, and even World War I, and there were picture albums and postcards that dated to the 1890s. The attic was a virtual altar of history.

As I rummaged through the detritus of history, feeling gripped by the zeitgeist of things gone, I came across an old newspaper with an article by Sidney Harris, a columnist for the Chicago Times. He had compiled a list of words for jobs and occupations that no longer existed, and he asked how many of us today could identify the jobs involved.

. . . broderer, cordwainer, fletcher, girdler, horner, lorimer mercer, pavior, chandler, tyler, poulter, salter, and skinner . . .

I did poorly on the test, but that fact drummed in the ephemeral nature of our livelihoods. Our jobs, crafts and even professions come and go and, pari passu, the words that went with them. Obsolescence is always looming around the corner as new technologies come to push to oblivion the old ways in a process that the Austrian economist Joseph Schumpeter called *creative destruction.* It isn't only words that die, but human dreams, the means of livelihood and the way of life of a people. The métier of one generation is rendered useless; it cannot be relayed to the next generation because it has been rendered useless, nullified by change.

By coincidence, minutes earlier I had seen a dusty contraption in the attic whose function had eluded me. It turned out to be a tapper for Morse code. I had seen this gadget in action in old movies about the American West when signals still traversed through wires, long before the radio. In those days this telegraph machine was on the cutting edge of communications; it easily beat the smoke signals or the pony express. Imagine how important the telegraph operator must have been. I can picture him as a railroad employee wearing a visor and a black string tie, deciphering the messages that came as squeaky pulses through the wires. Think of how indispensable he was in his day, as the only man who knew the alphabet of those dots and dashes. I could picture him receiving a message surrounded by people anxious to know what those ticks and pecks meant that only he knew. Only he could decipher those taps instantaneously; only he had the dexterity to ask questions and communicate with the operator on the other end. People crowded around him restlessly waiting to know the news. The world hung on his words. What happened? How many died? Is the worst over? What are they telling you? Tell us!

He was the Man of the Hour! I wonder how much he earned doing that. How long was his period of apprenticeship? What was his ranking in the economic pecking order and in the social scheme of things? But, in the end, what happened to him? How did he tumble from his peak? Did he go into the night of oblivion raging, kicking and screaming, or did he just fade away quietly as the radio superseded him?

Where is the blacksmith? Where are the appliance technicians, the TV and radio repairmen, the fixers and menders displaced by our throw-away society?

I went on to other things. I picked up a book that seemed to be an early precursor of the yellow pages. But it was an early mail-order catalogue from Sears. Its pages were full of drawings of old contraptions, appurtenances and appliances that have disappeared with the tides of time. There was a drawing of a clothes washer, a laundry tub with an attached clothes wringer with a hand crank. There were all sorts of manual implements, drills, windlasses, hoes, scythes, and winches, and there was also clothing—quaint, and dated, ridiculous apparel. Clothing is probably the most volatile category of society's fads. Women's fashions are among the first things to become dated and passé. Where now is the place for these discarded words?

The ruff, the corset, the bonnet, the stomacher, the tabard, the farthingale, the bloomers, and the knickerbockers.

I picked up another book. A World Atlas this time. Aha, I thought to myself, here is something that does not change. But even before I had opened the Atlas, I had corrected myself. How wrong I was to think that political geography would not change! The earth may not change, but the world goes through the convulsions of wars, revolutions, and changes in ideologies and political systems which change the maps as nations come and go. Political systems and economic systems change from monarchy to republics, from feudalism, to colonialism, utopianism, capitalism, Nazism and communism and with them the shape and name of countries. What ever happened to Siam, Bechuanaland, Rhodesia, Ceylon, or Dutch Guiana? While we slept, they became respectively: Thailand, Botswana, Zimbabwe, Sri Lanka and Suriname. Where are the biblical kingdoms now? Where is Philistia? Elam? Cilicia?

Words reflect the state of the world in all its aspects, in what people do, in the way they earn a living, in the things they use, in the things they wear, in the places they live, and in the way they think. My visit to that attic was becoming so sentimentally philosophical that I was unconsciously humming a tango.

But why a tango? When people in America think of tango, they think of music and dance only. But in Argentina (where tangos are from), tangos have lyrics and, oh, what lyrics they are! Tangos are poetry, philosophy, stories and essays. They are literature. Their lyrics cover the gamut of love in all its forms, unrequited, betrayed, denied, forgotten, misunderstood, scorned and much more. In fact, tangos have something to say about everything under the sun. Some are quite philosophical—especially those by Enrique Santos Discepolo (1901-1951). And quite a number of them are about things, ordinary objects—streets, walls, bachelor apartments, pampas, villages, guitars, trains, carnations, honeysuckles, bicycles, and just plain junk. There is, in fact, a very famous tango called *Cambalache* (junk) by Discepolo, in which junk serves as a metaphor for the Twentieth Century. Discepolo decries the modern world of his day, the roaring 1920s. It's going to the dogs, he says.

Tangos have a strong predisposition towards nostalgia. They often romanticize the old days. Some are odes, lofty requiems for cherished objects long gone. It was natural that as I rummaged through that attic, feeling soaked in the aura of the past that a particular tango would surface into my consciousness. The tango was "Casas Viejas" (Old Houses), dating to 1935, and written by another Argentinean lyricist-poet-philosopher, Ivo Pelay. I had been humming this tango distractedly and subconsciously for several minutes, but now it was playing more distinctly in my mind. It was no longer a hint of a melody, but a surging musical statement that tried in its own musical way to echo my thoughts about change and the tides of history. Then its lyrics came into my mind, reminding me of those cherished old houses that had been razed by the bulldozers to make way for the new, those houses that lived only in the heart of those sentimental souls that cherished them and missed them. The lyrics asked: does anyone remember those dear old houses that time blotted out? Answering its own questions, the lyrics lamented the docility with which the houses disappeared and went to their oblivion unceremoniously, "like cattle being herded to the slaughterhouse, without anyone telling them goodbye." That simile always gets me. I picture myself by the roadside watching that cow go by, wanting to give her something, some grass or some alfalfa. But I have none. A tear will have to do.

I picked up another book, an old dictionary this time, which made me think of why and how other words which are not about apparel or contraptions die, words such as those that Shakespeare used:

Fie, haply, perchance, vouchsafe, betroth, mislike, methinks, forslow, bruit, contumely, quietus, exeunt, opprobrium, puzzel.

Take the first of these, *fie*. Lovely little world. Why did *fie* have to die? Perhaps words roam away, resentful that they are being ignored, sensing that they are not wanted, fading from the scene, like homeless hobos. Death is never actually confirmed. Time just marches on, and the years bury the words in an absence of usage. Dictionaries seem to notice these lapses and make comments about them from time to time. If a word is absent from current print and can only be found in books that are over 50 years old, the word becomes MIA—except they don't call it that. Ultimately words become shadows of themselves, specters of the language of another era. Dictionaries take to calling them *archaic* and *obsolete* until, at some point, they give it the ultimate put down of silence and quit listing them altogether.

The dictionary I had picked up was in great disrepair. It had no cover or titular pages. I could not determine its age. It could have been 100 years old. It was a scruffy old book that had come unstuck. How ironic I thought, at one time this old book was brand new. It disdained the old words of its day and gave them short shift. But now he is an ancient relic himself. Dozens of new editions have buried him. What sort of a reception did it receive when it entered the gates of oblivion? Did the old words it had dismissed as passé come to haunt it? Surely, you have joined the rank of those dismissed words by now; and, surely, you have made your peace with them, now that you yourself have become an old, tattered curiosum, the skull of a book, a Yorick of a dictionary. Someone should write a tango about you.

# CHARADES AND KABUKI WORDS

---

**W**ords failed me that day—not because they were in my mind and refused to come out, but because I had none to give in Japanese. I was caught in a real-life situation, in a predicament where I was forced to play charades.

My wife and I were on a bus tour through Spain during September 1983. One early evening, after having toured the Alhambra all that day, we came into the dining room of our hotel and recognized a Japanese couple, fellow travelers in our tour. We had been traveling together for a few days but had never spoken to each other. This seemed like the perfect occasion to befriend them and get to know them. They were sitting at a table for four, with two empty chairs and we joined them. It was a friendly thing to do.

Then we discovered that they spoke no English. We sat there for a few minutes, exchanging silent pleasantries, smiles, bows, nods, silent toasts and bits of sign language. We were in that awkward period when we waited for the food to be served, thinking:

what next? The social weather at the table was changing from mostly quiet with scattered gestures, to uncomfortably odd.

Mr. Ito did speak a little English, but his wife spoke none. We knew from the tour director that he was a professor of something or other. We assumed he knew from the same source that we were professors also. In any case, even with the lack of communication, we felt the camaraderie of fellow souls.

We had arrived in Granada the night before, and on this day in early September we had toured the gardens of Spain and the Alhambra. We had worked up a good appetite walking and touring through the grounds leading up to the Generalife, the summer palace of Arab rulers that was built in the 1300s. The incline leading up to it was a shady alameda lined on both sides with cypresses and boxwoods. The gardens were laden with pergolas and lattices of manicured flowers and roses, hedges of myrtle, and giant structures of topiary. There were fountains everywhere. Running water was also part of the design of this manmade paradise that was started in pre-Columbian times when the Arabs still controlled Spain. There was the staircase of water cascading through a wall, and most memorable was the Patio de la Acequia with its rows of jets of water over a long thin canal making graceful arches that appeared to intertwine midway over the canal. The Spanish were so proud of the Generalife that they had taken this particular scene to adorn one of their bills, the 100-Peseta bill. On the other side of that bill was a picture of one of Spain's most renowned composers, Manuel de Falla.

While we sat at our dinner table, now half resigned to accept the awkward silence that turned us into mutes, music began to pour out of the loudspeakers with a timeliness that was heaven-sent. I recognized the crisp piano arpeggios that reminded me of water jets sparkling in the sunlight. The high notes captured in sound the splash of water drops colliding, like crystal chiming as it shatters, while the plaintive strings swept the air like a gentle, mellifluous wind. They were playing de Falla's piano concerto entitled Nights in the Gardens of Spain! De Falla had written this piece inspired by the beauty of the gardens, the very same gardens that the four of us at the table had toured that day. How appropriate, I thought. In my mind, I could picture the music bending the cypresses, rustling the gardens of the Generalife, swaying the plants in a delicate dance. That music took care of time for us at our dinner table. Those empty moments were now suffused with beautiful sounds that called for silence.

Except that now I wanted to share what I knew about the music with our Japanese friends. It would be a crime for them not to know the significance of the music they were hearing; how it tied to the things we had seen that day. I looked at them. They gave no inkling of knowing what was playing. And yet the music added so much to the total experience of being there. Ah, to be in Granada then, listening of all things to the movement entitled "In the Generalife"! I had to tell them. But how?

Then I remembered the Spanish peseta bill. I took my wallet out and searched through the bills to see if I had one and, aha, I did. I'd be a fool not to try to convey what was driving me insane to express. I had everything before me: pictures, sounds, and vivid memories of what we had just seen. I went for it.

I got their attention. I rolled up my sleeves a little and I pointed to the bill I had drawn from my wallet. The Japanese couple was drawn to my hands, observing them like children before a magician, their eyes wide-open with eager expectation. I am sure they thought I was going to perform a trick. Then I pointed to my ears and the air in the room, and I moved my hands and my fingers as if I were playing a piano. They seemed to get my meaning. They nodded their heads as if saying: The music, yes ... the music we are hearing...what about it?

Then I showed them the picture of de Falla on the bill and I mimicked more piano playing as I pointed to him. With gestures I told them: "This man you see here, yes? This man has something to do with the music playing in this room. He is the composer! He, he, he, he is it! He is it! And I didn't stop saying that till I got some confirmation from Mr. Ito that he got my meaning. His confirmation came soon with one of those vigorous Japanese eurekas: "Ah soooooooooo!"

Mr. Ito was excited. He borrowed my bill to show his wife and tell her what he had just learned. Then speaking in Japanese, for which I needed no translation, he pointed to the air in the room suffused by music, and he told her that we were listening to a piece of music that the man in the bill had composed. She beamed with delight and implicit understanding as if saying, how nice. Then she looked at me to acknowledge that she understood. They returned the bill to me with genuine appreciation on their faces. But there was more.

Now I wanted to tell them that the movement we were hearing, "In the Generalife," was named for the fountains and gardens which were pictured in the back of the bill. I started anew with a gesture that once again collected the music in the room with flair and led it with my hands into my ears. But this proved to be more difficult. They didn't catch my meaning. They seemed puzzled and confused. Was I repeating myself and making a mistake in the process? Was I flipping the bill to the wrong side? Who knows what they were thinking!

By pointing repeatedly, first to De Falla, then to the music in the room, and then to the picture of the Generalife on the other side of the bill, I kept working up the critical mass of the related objects, trying to light up meaning without words. It was as frustrating as rubbing sticks to make a fire. At one point Mr. Ito did convey something to his wife, but it lacked the magic flashpoint of understanding which had lit up his expressive face before. It didn't have that glorious confirmatory exclamation: "Ah, soooooo!" I'll never really know for sure what Mr. Ito told his wife.

I'll never know whether he fully understood the connection between the two sides of the bill, the music, the name of the movement, and the place we had visited.

But I took comfort in the thought that, surely, someday when back home in Japan, he might run across a book, or he might get a record of De Falla's music and then he might remember the evening when he heard his music in situ. Then, he might put it all together and then the charades of this forgotten stranger and his Kabuki words would finally hit their mark and light up meaning belatedly. Then perhaps, over space and time, Mr. Ito and I would finally finish our conversation.

# PIROPO WORDS

There is an age when War trumps Love in the heart of every boy, when a good war flick beats a romantic melodrama every time. That age caught me in the late 1940s in Guayaquil, Ecuador. My weekends were filled with war movies then. It didn't matter who the enemy was, Apache warriors, Japanese kamikazes, or goose-stepping Nazis. The only thing that mattered was the action, the gallantry, the courage, and the endurance of the war heroes. The Warfare could be naval, aerial, cavalry, or armored. I loved them all.

Monday should have been the worst day of the week as it meant going back to school. But strangely, Mondays were fun because we reminisced about the weekend movies, exchanging experiences, reliving the war action. I had two buddies in those days: Manuel and Alfredo the Chub. They were fellow roamers and wanderers who went to the same school and lived nearby. Although we were given money to ride the bus, we typically never rode it on the way home, spending the bus fare on candy instead, and walking home. We moseyed through the streets, horsing around, playing, and arguing—always arguing about the best movie, the greatest hero and the best branches of the military. We each had our preferences, but we would switch positions sometimes just to be ornery and to argue from another direction.

Great as all this was, it began to change gradually between our twelfth and thirteenth birthdays as another element (girls!) began to intrude upon our weekend fun and make the war movies secondary. Girls broke through the shell of innocence and led the way to a new age where boys opened their eyes and saw a marvelous world on the threshold of puberty, full of sweet awakenings.

At that early age we did not date as such. We did not pick up a girl at her house and take her to the movies. We simply met there. We gathered at the matinee before the show and paired there. Arrangements were orchestrated there, and things happened fast. Sometimes you met a girl for the first time, you chatted briefly and before you knew it, it was time to go in. She was your companion for the show. You sat together in what was a prelude to dating, the pre-teen date.

Of course, there were disappointments. It wasn't easy to end up with a girl, let alone one of your choice. Some girls came with chaperons; others were lost to boys bigger than you. Even at that early stage of philandering, there were braggadocios who claimed to be masters in the art of seduction. You had to have a line—so they said. The Spanish language has a specific word for this sort of thing. It is called a piropo. It is a blandishment, a sweet nothing; saccharine words you say to flatter the female and appeal to her vanity.

Most piropos were boilerplate, hackneyed little verses that one got from an older brother, from an uncle, or an older mentor. One went like this: "For just one look, I'd give a world. For a smile, Heaven itself would be too little. So, would you at least give me your name?"

Occasionally, these piropos proved disastrous. Some girls laughed and torpedoed your piropo with a blunt riposte such as: "That's the dumbest thing I ever heard." These girls, no doubt, had been coached by mean older sisters, or by protective mothers.

Fortunately, most girls were kind. They humored you along and when they turned you down, they did so gently. They excused themselves by saying something like: "My name is Lucrecia. But I cannot stay today, perhaps another time." Depending on how she said it, depending on her tone of voice, on the look of her eyes as she said it, she could leave you empty-handed, and yet, feeling rich because she left you with her lovely name, L-u-c-r-e-c-i-a. The name tickled your mouth and became a sweet melody in your heart. It played all week long, giving you something to look forward to until next weekend.

Little by little, it seemed that more and more Mondays were changing from talking about the movies, to talking about the girls. Real life was becoming more fun than the screen make-believe. I loved hearing these girl stories, the adventures or misadventures of the weekend. I wanted to know who got put down, and how. Had anyone come up with a new piropo? And had it paid off? Who did Manuel sit with? He was the one that usually scored. I wanted details.

"Manuel, Manuel. Did you hold hands with anyone yesterday?" I would ask impatiently. "And did you kiss her?"

Alfredo the Chub would tire of all this girl talk. He wanted to get back to the action in the movie and would ask, changing the subject, with great enthusiasm: "Hey, did you guys count how many Japanese Zeros that Navy ace shot out of the sky in the first five minutes?"

"Yes, three," I answered matter of fact and turned right back to Manuel to ask him: "What was her name, Man?" Alfredo the Chub continued on his own, making chortling machine-gun noises, rat-ta-tat as he shot at the imaginary Zeros. Then he would make other onomatopoeic sounds about the Zeros that fell in trails of smoke. "Pshew! YEEEEEEEEeeeeeh! Kaboom!"

One Monday, for once, we learned that Manuel had failed. He was so angry. He didn't want to talk about it, but we pressed him for details. This was special because he never failed. The big lover boy had fallen on his face. How wonderful for the rest of us klutzes! This was a tale worth hearing about. Even Alfredo the Chub found the accounting so titillating that he abandoned his aerial dogfight fantasies to help me coax the story out of Manuel.

"I didn't want to mess with that girl," Manuel began, "but she was a friend of my cousin Piedad, and Piedad wanted me to be nice to her. She wanted me to give her the full treatment: piropos and all, touching, kisses, the works. I finally agreed as a favor to my cousin because she's set me up well in the past and I was obliged. What can I tell you, that girl was a jerk from the get-go."

"What was her name?" Alfredo asked.

"Graciela Sanchez," Manuel replied tersely.

"Don't know her. Continue," said the Chub.

Manuel was upset even as he recounted the experience. "I knew I was going to have troubles with her from the start, when she removed her hand abruptly from the armrest the minute my fingers began crawling towards her. She was so skittish. This ain't gonna be easy, I thought to myself. So, I stared at her for a while as she sat there looking straight ahead at the screen, as in a trance, ignoring me. She really wasn't bad looking. I was getting inspired as I stared at her, and I remembered the words of that popular Mexican song, *Malagueña Salerosa*, which seemed fitting here. I whispered the words to her: 'What beautiful eyes you have under those gorgeous eyebrows.' And then, damn! Just as I said that la estúpida lowered her head to her lap and covered her face with her hands, like a little monkey who wants to see no evil, hear no evil, and see no movie. I wanted to pull her hair and punch her mug."

The Chub and I were rolling on the ground in hysterics, laughing wholeheartedly as we pictured the scene with la estúpida, but we had to get up and run away because Manuel started to kick the laughter out of us. Such were the antics of the new Mondays.


Weeks later came my turn. It began badly. I had just met a new girl outside the movie, a friend of somebody's sister this time -- can't even remember her name. We chatted briefly and I hoped that we would pair together. But she was carried off on some business and I ended up sitting alone next to Manuel and his steady girl. I consoled myself watching the movie, an American western about cowboys and Indians, Apache Broken Arrow, or some such.

I was sitting near the middle of the row, with several empty seats to my left when suddenly, to my surprise, I saw Alfredo the Chub walking up the aisle with a girl in tow. It was the girl I had met earlier. I signaled them to the seats on my left and she beamed as she recognized me and came to sit beside me, pulling Alfredo along.

The movie did not interest me one bit. From what I could tell, it did not interest her either. Only Alfredo the Chub was engrossed in it, counting falling Indians, fantasizing he had shot them. What a waste! The girl and I looked at each other every once in a while. Every time we did, we smiled as our eyes locked together; then, demurely we'd return our looks to the screen. At one point I rested my arm next to hers, touching it, and she did not move. What is this? I asked myself, half aflutter, my soul quaking inside me. Is this what I have been missing? Could this be my chance? Do I dare?

To be honest, I never believed in the effectiveness of piropos. I had a hunch that when a kiss was meant to be, it would happen without benefit of a piropo. If it was not meant to be, the piropo would be of no help at all. Besides, in the din of Indians wailing and carrying on, the horses neighing, the cavalry trumpeting for reinforcements and shooting, nobody could make out the words of a piropo. So why waste words? I wanted to say nothing, but that didn't seem right. That was not the proper protocol. But I couldn't just grab and smooch either. I dithered, not knowing what to do. There had to be a prelude, I thought. But where was it written that the words of the prelude had to be enunciated and understood? A mumble can speak volumes. A jumble of inarticulate facial pleadings with the right facial expression, could be just as effective as words. That was my plan: mumble your way through an unintelligible piropo.

I began. I moved my mouth as if saying something, but it was only nonsense syllables, and silent to boot. It was as if the time to pay had come, and I was using Monopoly money, tokens, and plug nickels. But, to my surprise, she was taking them! It was as if I lip-synched nonsense, and she applauded. I just mumbled random syllables, devoid of meaning, and she acted as if she understood them implicitly. Her eyes winked and twittered as if saying: "yes, yes, yes!" It was as if somehow, miraculously, I had pushed the right buttons, and the gates of heaven had opened.

My hands reached for her head and turned her face towards me, and then my lips found hers. We kissed. But I wasn't lifted towards heaven as I had expected. I tasted the unglamorous realities of a first kiss. And, like the first taste of many future addictions, it was not pleasurable. Like the first sip of beer, or the first puff of a cigarette, which were actually tortuous, this, too, was not pleasurable at all.

So, this is what kissing is all about... And to think I got it by cheating, by saying nothing at all. Then as our mouths twisted half opened, half closed, clashing and grating our teeth at times, the worst was yet to come. I got more than I wanted. I got what I didn't ask for. I got her chewing gum, and it was disgusting.

# LAST WORDS

---

September 11 has wounds that, even after several years, have not yet been cauterized. Every year when September comes around, I crash painfully into the 11th day. There is no soft landing. This day has become our generation's Alamo, the Pearl Harbor of the new millennium.

And yet, through the pain of recall, I find redemption in the memory of United Flight 93. This is the last plane to go down that day, the one that crashed in a field in Pennsylvania. It is also the only plane that communicated with the ground and learned what was happening; it is the only plane where the passengers fought back and thwarted the killers' plans; and it is the only plane that left us two inspiring unforgettable final words.

We shall never know if the passengers in the other planes knew what was happening before they died. But it is a matter of record that the passengers on United Flight 93 did know. They were in contact with friends and relatives on the ground. The record of their words is the legacy that serves as the antidote against so much loss and defeat for that day. The last words from this flight are like a rallying cry, like a trumpet blare to battle that put a stop to what would have been one more deadly success for the terrorists. Here, beginning with the chronology, are some of the facts that led to our moment of glory for that day.

8:46 a.m.: American Flight 11 hits the North Tower of the WTC
9:03 a.m.: United Flight 175 hits the South Tower
9:45 a.m.: American Flight 77 crashes into the Pentagon
10:10 a.m.: United Flight 93 crashes on a field in Pennsylvania.

To appreciate the significance of United Flight 93, let's put ourselves in the collective mind of Americans at 10 am, ten minutes before its crash, at a moment that marks the beginning of our deliverance from sheep-hood.

By 10 a.m. we knew the fate of the twin towers was foreclosed and it would be total destruction. By 10 a.m. we had learned that the warfront had expanded beyond New York to Washington. The Pentagon had taken a direct hit only minutes before and was in flames. By 10 a.m. United Flight 93 had not yet crashed. Its fate was only a conjectured possibility; it was the proverbial shoe we feared might still fall out of the sky. By 10 a.m. we still bobbed about in a sea of ignorance battered by a constant surge of unanswerable questions. We looked to the immediate past and to the immediate future equally perplexed. The past made no sense; it was incomprehensible, raising questions with no answers. Who? Why? How? The future brought its own anguish and uncertainty. Is it over yet? Could there be more? Where? When? We still had no answer to any of these questions.

Given the luck and success of the terrorists, we knew by 10 a.m. that anything was possible. The mayhem had not yet played out; there could have been more attacks; we had nothing under control yet. Even today, with perfect hindsight, I still gasp in disbelief at the flawless execution of the terrorists' mission. The question still rankles: Why, with so many steps to carry out and with so many possibilities for failure, why and how did they manage to sail so unerringly over all their hurdles? Success of such magnitude defies the laws of probability. To think they were able to demolish the twin towers using no explosives, firing no missiles, just brandishing box cutters. They pulled it off practically with their bare hands! Like something out of a cartoon, like a Rube Goldberg scheme that works disgustingly well against us.

The numbers alone were stacked against the killers. There were only four or five terrorists in each plane, against 80 to 100 passengers and crew. The terrorists could have been overpowered since they were basically unarmed. Why weren't they?

They weren't stopped because they were trying a brand-new trick in world history, one that was so perfidious that it camouflaged every satanic step and made them virtually invisible to us, impossible of being suspected. This was a colossal advantage to them. They knew everything about us, and we knew nothing about them. They took advantage of our innocence, our trust, and our goodwill. We were children playing against card sharks, lambs playing with wolves.

But time was their enemy. Eventually we would wise up. In fact, by the time United Flight 93 came around we had broken the hex and shattered the terrorists' shield of invincibility!

The terrorists knew our values, our thought processes, our beliefs and they knew that we did not know theirs. To them, our inability to grasp hatred as perfervid as theirs was a weapon in itself. They counted on the fact that no one could fathom the darkness of their intent. This bought them time and maneuverability; they could go about their business without any interference from us. Indeed, some passengers might have assisted them unwittingly. To the terrorists, we were as good as blind, deaf and dumb. We were cattle to the slaughterhouse with a bovine smile.

To begin with, the terrorists passed themselves off as skyjackers. And everyone knows that skyjackers usually want money, or free transportation to a country of their choice. For certain, everyone assumed that they wanted to live. Nobody could have imagined that they wanted to kill themselves.

The terrorists fooled everyone, not only the people on the planes but on the ground as well. For example, the personnel on the ground thought nothing of the fact that the terrorists, with their Arabic names and passports bought one-way tickets and paid with cash. They just couldn't pull that off today. The terrorists carried box cutters into the planes with impunity, knowing that no one could suspect anything. What harm could anyone possibly do with box cutters? The terrorists knew that the pilot's cabin was not impregnable. The manufacturers had made the cabin accessible, thinking perhaps that no rational human being would ever want to harm the crew that could land them safely. The terrorists knew there were no armed sky marshals on the planes. They would not have been necessary against the usual skyjackers. So, the terrorists saw no impediments. Their operation would be a shoo-in, a piece of cake.

How much the world has changed since then! We can now look back and see the dirty game the terrorists were playing, and we can see the way they cheated. They had a trump card which to our minds was unthinkable. That card was their own death, their own sacrificial suicide. We didn't know, couldn't know, that they didn't mind dying, as long as they succeeded in killing us.

Who could have conceived that there could be no negotiating in their deadly game? We had nothing to negotiate with. Their own life meant nothing to them; it was no bargaining chip. They didn't want it. They came prepared to die.

This notion of suicide as weapon was completely new to us then. The Kamikazes of WWII are a rough equivalent, but they are not comparable because those were tactical ploys during raging battles during an ongoing very brutal war. This attack took place in blue skies during peace time against innocent civilians with no possible tactical military aim. It was totally unexpected.

If it is hard for us to understand this type of crime even now, imagine how inconceivable it would have been then. I can imagine how our innocence played out in those first two planes. Perhaps some passengers were alarmed by the scuffling and groaning in the cabin. Perhaps they wanted to take action, but they talked themselves out of any heroics, thinking that it was better to negotiate. Just give them what they want. Take them wherever they want to go. Let's get this over with in a civilized way.

The passengers might have settled down to wait for word from the pilot, not knowing that the pilot was already dead or dying from a slit to his throat with a box cutter, and not knowing that the plane was already under the control of a suicidal maniac who was (and this would have been impossible to believe at the time) capable of flying the plane himself. At that point one of the terrorists may have emerged from the cockpit. He would have been a clean-cut and close-shaven young man with American clothes that made him look like a graduate student, a hard-working and budding intellectual who wouldn't hurt a fly. He would address the passengers, trying to allay their fears by assuring them, (by lying actually), that they were going to be okay.

"Please, please! Stay calm. Remain seated. Everything is under control. Nothing is going to happen to you."

At the sound of his reassuring words, the passengers would calm down and comply, sitting back down, trusting him and feeling grateful for his assurances. How nice of him. The passengers would settle back to wait patiently, expecting that the conflict in the cockpit would be resolved amicably and rationally. Seconds later, however, they would all die engulfed in a ball of fire, but in blissful ignorance of their killers' lust for death. Some of the passengers might still have had in their mind the image of the kind soft-spoken young man that had just come out to assure them that everything was going to be okay.

A similar scene would play out minutes later on the plane that was headed for the other tower of the World Trade Center. By the terrorists' good planning the attacks would be executed as simultaneously as possible, without delays between one plane crash and the next, so as to avoid alerting us, and breaking our spell of ignorance and victimhood.

But they can't have it all perfect. Nature is not that accommodating. Their good luck runs out. They are exposed in the end. By 10 a.m. more than an hour had elapsed from the time of the first plane crash. It is not clear how much the passengers on United Flight 93 might have learned from talking to people on the ground through the in-flight telephones. Perhaps they learned of the hecatomb of the Twin Towers by then. Perhaps they aged 100 years already in those few minutes, as the rest of us had by 10 a.m. What is known is that they fought back, and they managed to foil the terrorists' plans. This plane crashed in a field in Pennsylvania and did not reach its intended target, which might have been either the U.S. Capitol, or the White House.

Some of the passengers on United Flight 93, fearing that there would be no walking out alive from that plane decided to act. But the dawning of one's imminent death does not necessarily drive one to heroic actions instantly. The person is bombarded with conflicting emotions and frantic arguments that urge him to do something, but also caution against doing anything rash. Instincts urge one thing; reason cautions against it. "Wait! Not yet. Don't be in a rush to die. You can't do anything once you are dead. Think! Watch what you do." At the same time, another voice just as compelling cries out for action. "Get up! You don't have much time. It is not a question of survival anymore. You are going to die. The question is how. These bastards have taken control of the plane, and they are going to try to crash it on a city, Washington D.C. most likely, in order to kill as many people as possible. You can prevent that. Don't let them get there. Crash it now while you are still flying over the countryside. Save some lives down below."

Eventually the voices of caution are quelled—they cannot stall action any longer. The blinders are off the victims' eyes. The shackles of innocence are broken; the jig is up. The big secret of the terrorists is out. They can no longer fool people; they can promise nothing, and they can demand nothing in return. The only thing at issue is death, but death on whose terms? The passengers now see the skyjackers for what they really are: Islamic fanatics, suicidal killers out to consummate a death orgy. And they have no guns.

From reports by Newsweek and other sources, one passenger on United Flight 93, Todd Beamer, is known to have been in communication with people on the ground. What he learned from the ground is not nearly as important as what he told the ground. His words are the rallying cry of the first and final battle of that day. He and those who fought with him were the first Americans to resist and "not go gently into that bad night." As he closed off, he gave every indication that he knew what had to be done. And he was up to it. The rest is history. His last words were:

"Let's roll!"

# WORD FAIR

In awe, like a child at an amusement park, I was walking through the streets of Word Metropolis, the Mecca for word lovers. I had come to attend a convention on words and language. I was gawking at the canyons of skyscrapers that lined the offices of publishing empires on my way to the Merriam Webster, the big hotel that was hosting the Word Conference this year, an event so especial, so unusual that it was like Word Expo, and Word Olympics all combined.

Words came to this gathering as athletes go to the Olympics, as young women go to Miss Universe beauty pageants. There are parades where words march in stanzas, with cadence, in rhyming couplets, carrying banners of poetic titles. Words come to perform in oratory, to be seen, to be heard, to titillate the intellect. There are activities for every taste. For popular culture there are contests, game shows, parades, and fashion shows. For the intellectuals there are academic discussions, paper presentations, debates, and oratory. The linguists and lexicologists, the etymologists and the philologists all came to discuss the latest trends in vocabulary, the latest buzzwords, and the latest neologisms. Everyone was anxious to learn what new words had come up over the year. Rumors had it that we've had a bumper crop of new words this year. More strangely, there were rumors that old, ancient words would make their eerie appearances, defying credulity for their longevity. They are the word equivalent of mummies, of Dracula-like old creatures that rise from crypt-like books and come alive after sleeping for centuries and millennia. Two of these, so I was told, *anadiplosis* and *anaphora* were from the Golden Age of Greece, and they would be performing live tonight, speaking in verse while adhering to the particular structure that defines them. I had bought tickets for that performance. Wouldn't miss it for the world.

Outside the hotels there was a carnival atmosphere. The streets had been turned into pedestrian malls. The sidewalks had been taken over by vendors with their stalls selling souvenirs and trinkets. There were makeshift theaters where performances were staged. The liveliness and the raunchiness gave it a circus quality, without the big animals. The place was alive with activities that exuded fun and good times. The sideshows were cleverly advertised and enthusiastically promoted by hustlers who barked their wares with gusto. I enjoyed listening to their spiel.

As I walked the streets, I noted some activity going on in the side alleys also. I suspected that there might be clandestine operations going on there. Incidentally, porno words and dirty talk were not allowed inside the big hotels. The seedy stalls had to operate outside and had to be able to run on a moment's notice in case the police raided them for violating city ordinances. This is where you could find the sex toys, the sex paraphernalia and sex vocabulary. This is where you would find the myriad synonyms for genitals, twat, quim, cunt, dong, putz, schlong. If you weren't into that sort of thing, you might still find the vocabulary amusing, the dildos, the Bobs, the simulator-stimulators. The porn magazines were interspersed between the volumes of ribald literature so you could ogle and peruse clandestinely under a proper cover. There was quite a variety of dirty books, scatological humor, sexy lewd short stories with accompanying glossaries for the uninitiated and assorted manuals with the latest raunchy slang. Who knows what other evil lurked there? For the time being I decided to suppress my curiosity about these dark alleys and check out the well-lit sidewalk shows. Just ahead of me was a man barking his heart out and I stopped to hear him.

"Hurry! Hurry! Hurry, Ladies and Gentlemen! Step right in and see the exotic creatures, the Janus words, the palindromes, the double-headed hydras, the Siamese twins; watch with your own eyes the homonyms, the heteronyms and the great homophones. They come in all sizes, everything from the monosyllabic to the sesquipedalian. We have puns, mondegreens, acronyms, crossword puzzles, acrostics and other word games. Get your tickets now for the most impressive collection of specimens ever seen in North America. Hurry, hurry, hurry!"

I walked a little farther and from behind the walls of make-do curtains I could hear someone spinning off homographs.

*He had a farm that produced produce*
*The dump was so full that it had to refuse refuse*
*What did the dove do when he got shot at? The dove dove.*

From the next stall I could hear PARAPRODOSKIANS being advertised. These are figures of speech in which the latter part of a sentence is surprising or unexpected. Here are a few well known examples:

*If I agreed with you, we'd both be wrong.*
*War does not determine who is right, only who is left.*

*To steal ideas from a person is plagiarism. To steal from many is research.*

*A clear conscience is a sign of only one thing: a fuzzy memory.*

*Where there's a will, there's relatives.*

*The last thing I want to do is hurt you. But it's still on my list.*

*A lass on high heels fell on her back and everyone saw ... she couldn't walk well with heels*

Ah, such wit. I loved these shows. So, I kept walking, getting samples from each. I then came to a gentleman sitting on a throne-like highchair—like a shoe-shine get-up. He fancied himself a word magician and was wearing a silk outfit and a turban. He was giving a test. We were supposed to guess what the following words had in common.

*BANANA, POTATO, DRESSER, GRAMMAR, REVIVE*

I tried and tried, but I couldn't guess their trick. To get the answer, he would come down and let me look into his stereopticon for five dollars. I was really stumped and curious, so I gladly paid the price. The itch to know was becoming unbearable. This is what I read in his gadget:

"Think of each of these words as a little choo-choo train. Now take the engine, (the first letter), and put it behind like a caboose. BANANA becomes ANANAB. The engine now pushes the train instead of pulling it. If you read it from right to left, it becomes the original word again. It works the same for the other words.

Wow! Imagine that! This is really word magic. I came to the next stall. They were playing a question-and-answer game. It went like this:

*What does a serial writer have for breakfast?* Cereal.

*How can a poor prophet get rich?* By making a profit.

*Where does a gentleman learn his good manners?* At the manor.

*Why couldn't Paul Revere talk when he got off his horse?* He was hoarse.

*What did Bambi call his mom?* Mother deer.

*

### The Bar of Intellectuals.

I made my way to the hotel where Anadiplosis and Anaphora would be performing. I went down to the bar. It was a dimly lit tavern in the basement where it was difficult to recognize a familiar face. I got a bottle of water and went for a place to sit. People were congregated in parties of different sizes, some standing, others sitting; the largest party had a dozen people and seemed to be a few drinks ahead of everybody else. They were talking loudly and freely, enjoying themselves, even singing at times. I moseyed my way in their direction and plumped down on a cushy chair not far from them.

Although I could find no one I knew, I did not feel displaced or lonely. The place inspired the gregariousness of fellow feeling. A warm spirit of camaraderie permeated the ambience and made me feel at home among perfect strangers. After all, everyone in that bar shared a love of words. The people there had either common métiers, or common avocations, all dealing with words. There were lexicologists, philologists, grammarians, etymologists, linguists, language teachers, English teachers, rhetoricians, writers, dramatists, poets, versifiers, poetasters, limerick spinners, lyricists, satirists, and semanticists—not to mention spoonerists and punsters, word gamesters, the people who do acrostics, anagrams, antigrams, and finally, the scrabble champions and crossword puzzle makers.

While I felt safe and unthreatened, I was curious about the people around me. I kept asking myself: What sort of people are they? Do they have homes to go back to—wives, husbands, children, or pets—like normal people? Or do they just live for this in this world of conventions, lecturing and talking—today in New York, tomorrow in Chicago, and then Toronto? How often do they do this? For me this sort of thing was good for only about once every four years. As I mused about the people, examining their body builds and their complexions, I noted that most of them looked like bookworms—they had that sedentary out-of-shape look, or that Gothic nocturnal look of inveterate readers. None of them seemed athletic, or outdoorsy. Strange thoughts went through my mind.

Aha, I thought, maybe these are the weird words that take human form, bizarre creatures akin to ghosts or vampires, who live in crypts, in ancient books that no one reads anymore. They date to Greece's golden age. They come alive only in these conventions or in the arcane halls of academe. As soon as this conference is over, they will vanish from view and transform themselves into words again, returning to the pages of their books which, in their absence, would have been full of blank spaces, like unmade empty beds, or like body-hollowed empty coffins. Upon reaching their resting places, they would pull the book covers over themselves like a coffin-lid and sleep for months or years till the next convention.

After a while my eyes became accustomed to the dark. I could discern more details from people. They were no longer silhouettes and shadows. I could distinguish hair color and skin complexion. Looking in the direction of that large group sitting around a big table, I was struck by how strange the people looked. The men looked as if their names might have been Litotes, Synecdoche, or Zeugma. The women were thin, almost anorexic, theatrical in dress and makeup. I wanted to go nearer and touch them or pinch them to see if they had warm human flesh.

This is ridiculous, I told myself. Words in the guise of people! Come on! And to think, you have only been drinking water. I began to think that they weren't words at all but honest-to-goodness human beings, thespians absorbed by the appearance of the characters they portrayed, ancient Aegean types. Poetry and literature suffused the air. I began to catch the bug. I started thinking in rhyme. That's how powerful the aura was. One of these, a woman in her mid-forties stood up and began to speak. I could swear she was speaking in poetry, versifying in lines that had a certain lilt, linking the first word of a line with the last word of the previous line. This has got to be Ana Dee, I told myself (that being the nickname I had given Anadiplosis). I was sure of it. Before I knew it, I was soliloquizing in rhyme myself. That infectious sense of poetry had gotten to me. I could just imagine a dialogue in rhyme with her that went like this.

I can tell who you are by what you said.
Is your name Anadiplosis by any chance?
"No, you've confused me with Anaphora, I am afraid.
We do resemble each other at first glance."

Ah, how silly of me to confuse Ana Phi for Ana Dee.
With them you can't just go by what you see.
You have to go by sound in order to tell
You have to listen and listen well.
There's no problem with Anaphora and Anadiplosis.
But what about Zeugma, Metonymy, Aposiopesis?
How does Antonomasia and Anastrophe
Differ from Litotes, Synecdoche and Apostrophe?

Gradually, the din toned down and I could hear her very well. There was indeed a pattern to the words the speaker was intoning. Her talk was like a choreographed speech. She spoke in lines that fell and rose again with an undulating lilt, an ebb and flow. Ah, this has to be Ana Dee, the queen of relay, the reiterative Grand Dame. This is what she was saying:

*In years to come when you remember this*
*This scene will seem to be a dream*
*A dream in the fog of a memory*
*A memory you will assail with questions,*
*Questions of who was who? What was what?*
*What was I doing there? Was I awake?*
*Awake but half stoned? Or was I asleep?*
*Asleep but dreaming that I was awake?*
*Well, whatever this is, whatever we are*
*We are all entitled to wild imaginings,*
*Imaginings about words parading as people,*
*People being words, and nonsense such as that,*
*That we were ancient tropes, that we were alive,*
*Alive but relegated to a corner of language which is practically lost*
*Lost to the modern world, except for happy nights*
*Nights such as tonight when we get a new lease on life among friends*
*Friends that still know who we are and what we mean.*
*But, alive or not, whether word or person, here I am.*
*I am here to bring back the glory of a style*
*A style of poetry that is lost*
*Lost from the scene, except for a few lines*
*Lines such as these which I hope will be used again*
*Again and again till they flow freely*
*Freely and naturally from the lips of poets*

*Poets who remember me. So, raise your glasses and drink.*
*Drink not to me, but to the concept, to the idea,*
*To the idea I stand for, my concatenating lines*
*Lines that end, but then ratchet themselves to go on*
*On and on to a new beginning, to a new line, refusing to end*
*To end, as I reluctantly resolve to do now.*


Wow! People loved it. They were applauding her with a standing ovation. I had guessed correctly. She was Anadiplosis. I felt lucky to be so near her, but not near enough to address her personally and shake hands. I felt as if Ana Dee had been speaking to me, addressing me and perhaps taking me to task for my thoughts and my questions, which she could read as well as if I had articulated them aloud. Was she real? Was her blood warm? Who cares! She personified what she stood for, and she did it with charm. That's what mattered.

Then Anaphora, (Ana Phi to me) began to speak. She resembled Ana Dee. They looked as if they were close kin. She, too, was swarthy, Mediterranean and thin. When people settled down and when the din hushed, she began to speak.


*We live a dream, believing it is real*
*We live reality as if it were a dream.*
*Who can say what is real, what is not?*
*Who can tell real life from fiction,*
*When at times the theater mimics life*
*When at times life is pure theater?*
*Words, however, function in both*
*Words retain their meaning in fact or fiction.*
*Here we are then to affirm their constancy*
*Here we are to prove their virtual immortality.*
*After the stagehands have died*
*After the audience, actors and playwrights have left*

*All that remains is the play and, more explicitly,*
*All the words in the play.*
*Words are the blood of eternal life, spoken, written, read, or acted*
*out*
*Words whispered or shouted; words sworn to and then broken.*

*"Clothes," the haberdasher will tell you,*
*"Clothes make the man. But clothes do not the man make.*
*Words make the man!*
*Words make the man when he is alive, and*
*Words recall the man when he is dead*
*Words, always words.*
*Shakespeare has been dead so long now, and yet*
*Shakespeare is so alive, so close to us now.*
*His words live on, and he lives through his words*
*His words throb in our hearts and echo in this chamber*
*Doubt that the stars are fire*
*Doubt truth to be a liar*
*And like the stars his words forever shine*
*And like the truth his words immortalize the man*
*This much is certain*
*This much I believe*
*So long as men can breathe, and eyes can see*
*So long his words give joy to me and thee.*

There was thunderous applause. Ana Dee hugged Ana Phi. We all rejoiced with good cause, toasting the Anas from Delphi. They hugged and gave each other high fives as people mobbed them and huddled around. There was no question they were very much alive. Ana Dee and Ana Phi were hale and sound.

I would have loved to wish them well in person, but the fans made an impenetrable loop around them. I went for another water bottle and walked for a spell. On my return I had to sit by another group because my seat had been taken and I found a new place by a professor holding court with graduate students. Their enthusiasm showed on their eager faces. I sat nearby and prudently eavesdropped.

*

### *The Literature Class.*

While I sat within ear reach of the class, I kept looking around to see if I found someone I recognized. I was not looking for anyone I knew personally, but just somebody in the news, somebody I've seen on magazines or on TV, contemporaries of the current scene, someone like William Safire of "nattering-nabobs-of-negativism" fame; or someone like Richard Lederer of Anguished English; or like James Kilpatrick, the syndicated curmudgeon judge of current English usage; perhaps Dr. Mardy of chiasmus fame. I felt sure I would recognize someone before long. But I never did.

I could hear the group sitting behind me very well, and by turning my head slightly I could also see them. The professor was talking to his young students, commenting on the words of Ana Phi and Ana Dee. He was saying:

*Thus, in the end, physical matter does not matter.*
*Spiritual, intellectual matter—which is not matter—matters.*
*We die, and our words go on living, proving that*
*The pen is not only mightier than the sword*
*But mightier even than the matter we're made of.*

The speaker continued elaborating on the undying value of words, adding: "Our words in effect consecrate our immortality. And this is something that writers should certainly take to heart. Therefore, watch what you say, and mean what you say. Go over your words twice. You don't want to be remembered by words that you regret you ever said. When in doubt, quote others. By the way, did you all notice how Ana Phi paraphrased those lines from Hamlet? 'Doubt that the stars are fire…Doubt truth to be a liar.' I thought her allusion to Shakespeare was inspired and on the mark."

"Yes, I loved that," said a young woman in agreement. "The bard of the ages rose to the occasion for the millionth time. She didn't even have to say his name. We would have known it by pure antonomasia."

"By what did you say?" asked a young man sitting next to her.

"Antonomasia."

The young man seemed to be taking notes as she spoke. The young woman explained: "That is a word or phrase that fits a person by acclaim, by reputation, or infamy; it fits so well that it becomes synonymous with his name. If I say, for example, 'The Prince of Darkness' or the 'King of Rock and Roll' who do you think of by antonomasia?"

"Dracula, Elvis?"

"Exactly."

The professor then addressed another member of the group. "What about you, Craig? You've been sitting quietly tonight. Do you have any observations on what was said?"

"Well, I thought I caught an anastrophe."

"Really? Where? When?" asked another young woman quite excited.

"It was when Ana Phi said: 'Clothes do not the man make.'"

"Yes, of course, instead of 'Clothes do not make the man.' Gosh, that flew completely over my head! It was so natural at the time she said it that I didn't think anything of it."

"That's the point," interrupted the professor. "That's the way it's meant to be when you do it right. The flow of words should be so free and unstrained that you are not bothered by their unusual transposition."

Then the young man who had been taking notes coughed and raised his hand to catch the professor's attention.

"Sir, I think I caught a 'metanamee,'" he said timidly.

"Metonymy," corrected the professor in a gentle way.

"It was when you said, 'the pen is mightier than the sword.'"

"Did I say that? That is such a cliché. I am embarrassed to own up to it. But, yes, that's good. You got me, Joe. That is a metonymy."

"Did you also have a chiasmus, sir?" asked the first young woman.

"If I did, it was perfectly unintentional, and I can't remember it. Pray tell us where and when."

"It was when you said something like: 'Matter may matter now, but what matters when matter no longer matters, was never matter.'"

"Oh, thank you dear. But I never said it as well as that. It sounds better and more chiastic the way you put it."

Then Craig wanted to ask a question. "What advice would you give us about acquiring words and being up on all these esoteric terms? If there was one single thing you would recommend, what would that be?"

"Read!" the professor flashed back. "Tire your eyes reading! Travel the world through words. Turn the pages, as if every page were a new adventure. Read. Read. And read. And from the safety of your armchair, experience vicariously the adventures and mis-adventures that others have gone through. Learn—without spending money on traveling, and without even moving from the comfort of your seat—about worlds that are far beyond your horizon, and perhaps beyond the reach of your lifetime. But as you read, take time to savor the words, for they are the servers that transport you across the byways of the worlds you cover. Stop to know better the strangers that serve you so well; communicate with them as you would chat with your jungle guide, your ferryman, the Sherpa, the taxi driver, your rickshaw puller, or your gondolier. They know their environs so well and can add color and history to the trajectory. Give words their due and look them up. Under no circumstances ignore a word that is knocking at your door. Let her in. Resist the impulse of proceeding with your reading when you don't know the meaning of a word, thinking that you can infer its meaning from context. Such laziness will enslave you to permanent ignorance. Jot the word down to look it up later, but don't ignore it. It may take more time, but it's well worth it. And while you are looking up a word, take the time to delve a little into its etymology, into its affinity with other words, into its correct pronunciation, and into its connotations. You'll get more out of the miles traversed that way. Invest your money in good unabridged dictionaries. You are all beyond the pocket size ones now."

Suddenly, there was a commotion in the room. I could hear hollering from the upper floor and people rushing down the stairs trying to get away from the uproar. All the lights came up in the bar. Suddenly, it looked like a stadium at a night game. The exit doors swung wide open, and people rushed out. I went up to investigate. It turned out to be an altercation, a scuffling between a man and the hotel's security guards. An angry man was shouting, protesting the fact that this hotel had denied lodging to some words that it considered vulgar. In particular, the f-word had been thrown from the premises. According to the man, the hotel was discriminating against the word on moral grounds and a dictionary does not have the right to do that. It cannot pick and choose, especially if it claimed to be *unabridged,* as this one did. You don't have the right to do that, you so-and-so, the man was shouting as the police dragged him out.

I woke up and tried to write down all that I had heard and seen during this wonderful evening in the world of words before I forgot it.

# BAD WORDS

In my youth, I worked in the lab of an industrial plant, doing chemical analysis. One evening I was multi-tasking at warp speed doing five different things at once, when someone from another department phoned, demanding his test results. When I told him they weren't ready, he blew up, accusing me of loafing on the job. I blasted him with a barrage of insults and hung up.

Cussing occurred daily at this plant. Profanity was the linguistic sauce du jour, the *lingua franca* that helped us get through the work stress. People thought nothing of it. They returned fire with fire, bad with bad, and that was that. Nothing much came of the vitriolic exchanges. I was, therefore, surprised when at the end of the shift, the man I had insulted on the phone came into my lab, offended by my words. He was fuming. I remember his eyes had a glassy watery film, like those of an angry cobra.

"What was that you called me?" he demanded to know as he looked at me, scorching me with his stare. I said nothing, pretending to be busier than I really was, going about my chores, putting pipettes away, turning off Bunsen burners, and straightening out the lab for the next shift.

"What was that you called me?" He repeated for a second time, daring me to repeat it, getting louder and more threatening.

I had the good sense not to accept his dare and repeat my insults. He would have pulverized me. Besides, I did not know which of my insults had hurt him so much. I had thrown so many at him at once. So, to end the impasse honorably, I apologized for all my bad words. "I am sorry about my words. Anger gets the best of us here. We are under a lot of stress. But don't take it so badly. Whatever I said were just words to blow off steam and nothing more. Don't read more into that. If my words offended you, I take them back. I'm sorry."

He did not like my apology. He pounded his fist on my counter, shouting: "Break it down, damn it! Break down what you called me, goddamn it!"

Break down what? I asked myself, puzzled. What's there to break down? Insults are just bombasts, fiery air with thistles and burs, not declarations of fact. How ridiculous can he get!

Fortunately for me, he had come with his work partner, Vick, who was more conciliatory.

"Come on Jack," said Vick, "you've done told him, and he's done apologized. Let's go."

I looked at Vick thankfully, glad that he was there. Silently I pleaded for him to calm down his monster friend and take him away.

But Jack was still furious, doggedly persisting that I parse my sentences and heft the meaning of each word. It took me a while to learn that what galled him so much was that I had called him a son of a bitch. And horror of horrors, to him that meant that I thought his mother was a bitch. Everything else he could take, but he had no antidote for that one; it grated inside him and drew blood. It was as if I had called his mother a bitch to her face. He was that literal.

I wanted to tell him that his mother's virtue was the farthest thing from my mind. I could easily accommodate him by leaving his mother out, and going after his dad, calling him a faggot's bastard. But this was no time to be sarcastic. The only way to appease him was by saying I had not meant to malign his mother. Amazingly, that's what he wanted to hear. That's what it took to calm him down. He left my lab. Whew!

How literal can you get? How humorless? I wonder if he knew that siblings call each other sons of bitches sometimes. Could he see the irony in that? The insult should boomerang, but it doesn't. Reality and common sense thwart the harm. Siblings are inoculated against the literal venom of the expression. Expletives are nothing more than incantations, a brew of words we spew out to let off steam. The evil delight in enunciating it does provide relief. Insults are meant to hurt, but never to main or kill. I've never known anyone who took so much umbrage. He acted as if my barbs were real swords and spears that crisscrossed his body and turned him into a suffering Saint Sebastian.

I did not have more dealings with him after that; the few times we did, the communication was bland business talk.

"Do you have my saponification numbers?"

"Yes, they were in range," I said as I gave him the numbers.

"Fine," he would say and hang up.

A few months later I quit that job to finish college and never gave that place a second thought until one fateful day two years later when I was visiting home on Spring break. I saw a big spread on the newspaper about a homicide/suicide. I couldn't believe my eyes as I read the particulars. Jack had discovered that his wife had been having an affair with, of all people, his work partner, Vick. He had blasted them both with a shotgun and then killed himself.

The newspaper burned my hands as if it was on fire. Then through the slithering dancing flames I could see those glassy cobra eyes, staring at me.

# CHAPTER XI

# FIRST WORD: MAMA

A lice sat in a rocking chair, holding her six-month-old baby in her lap, wondering when he would learn to say the word *mama*. Does this happen naturally, instinctively? At what age exactly do they learn it? She should have known this by now. She had two older girls, but in their case, it had all happened so naturally. She couldn't recall how long it took for them because she hadn't been concerned about it. She remembered only that very soon after her girls learned the word, they opened the gates of speech. But her baby boy, Tony, would have a harder go of it because he had had problems and had special needs. She was anxious about him. Perhaps, for his sake, she should not wait for nature but should help it along.

She stroked his hair, combing it gingerly with her fingers and she started drilling him on the basic M-sounds, puckering her lips as she mimicked a cow mooing. "Mmmm, mom! Mmm, ma! Mmm, Mama! Mama! Mama! Maaamma!" When she wasn't drilling him on the phoneme, she would be talking to him in a sort of therapeutic soliloquy.

"Now look at Mommy, Sweetie, and listen," she would say as she anchored his tender little body in her lap so as to face her. "I want you to learn to recognize the sound of my voice. You don't need to understand what I'm telling you. That will come later. You just need to get used to the sound of Mommy's voice and remember it, distinguish it from that of the other people you've been hearing lately, the strangers, the doctors, and nurses. I want my voice to stand out above those. And, ah, look at me, too, my Sweet Darling. I want you to learn to recognize my face as well. This is your Mama . . . see? I will be in orbit around you, like your own private moon, watching over you always because you are the center of my universe. Yes sirree, that's what you are to me! Oh, yeah!"

The baby was quiet and did not move much. He was not as vivacious as most babies are at that age. He had been hurt, but it was difficult to assess the extent of his injuries and handicaps. Nobody knew for a fact whether he could see or hear. But Alice dismissed those concerns. She saw him through maternal eyes that were so deeply steeped in hope that it filtered out all dismal scenarios. To her, he looked as normal as could be expected, a little slow perhaps, somewhat sluggish, she admitted, but otherwise normal. She looked at his eyes and she could see that they moved; to her it seemed that he was taking in the room with his eyes. And, yes, he did make baby sounds. He cried at times. What more do they want? He'll be all right; she would tell herself.

"Oh, Sweetie, one of these days you will surprise us all by saying 'Mama'. I hope it will be soon. I would give worlds to hear you say it. On that day I will go mad with joy. I will run up and down like a crazy lady yelling: Hey, listen! My baby just said 'Mama,' his first word! Do you people know what that means? It means he's set the record straight about a lot of things. It means he's proved you wrong. It means my prayers have been answered. You people out there: doctors, nurses, state officials, lawyers and judges, did you get that? Oh, Baby, I'm telling you, that one little word would shake the world for us. What a wonderful day that would be. It would prove that you can hear; that you can speak; that you can think and that your little brain is fine. But hush now. Here comes Mildred."

Mildred, a woman in her mid-50's, came into the room followed by several children. She was a foster mother, registered with the state to provide childcare in her home. The children in her care were all wards of the state, and baby Tony was her youngest. Alice stood up now and kissed her baby one more time, adding: "Well, my Love, time goes by fast when you are having fun. Mommy must go now. Ms. Mildred's come already. But Mama will be back tomorrow. Yes, she will. Count on it."

Alice handed her baby to the foster mother and left. It was exactly two o'clock when she reached her car. As she turned on the ignition, the radio came on automatically, blaring aloud the theme music of a news program. At the top of the news—just as it had been for days—was the plight of a woman who had suffered brain damage and had lived in a vegetative state for 15 years. Now a battle was raging between her husband who wanted to let her die, and her parents who fought to keep her alive. Alice listened for only a few seconds and then she could take no more of the Terri Schiavo case. The incessant reporting of this case annoyed her. She was tired of hearing about it, and she turned off the radio with a brusque slap on the power button.

On the fateful day of the accident, she had left the baby in the care of her husband, the baby's father, while she was at work. The husband had lost his footing while holding the baby and had fallen on the floor on top of him. Baby Tony had lost his breath and turned blue, whereupon the father panicked and shook the baby in a desperate and ill-advised attempt to revive him. The baby wouldn't respond. The poor man ran out screaming and crying as he went into the street. A neighbor across the street came out to help; she applied mouth to mouth resuscitation and managed to restart the baby's breathing; then she called an ambulance. Thus began three weeks of hellish existence for the Stewart family.

The father was charged and remained in the custody of the authorities for a few hours. Even to this day the district attorney has not decided whether to prosecute him on grounds of child abuse. That is still pending. The baby, who remained in the hospital for over a week after the accident, is now a ward of the State of Kansas and remains in the care of Mildred Watkins. Andrew and Alice had to move heaven and earth to be near the baby; they had to break a lease and move 40 miles closer to Salina, Kansas. In the eyes of the authorities the parents were guilty, guilty of something—at the very least of negligence, or carelessness. They were not off the hook. Fortunately, the small community in which the Stewarts lived was very sympathetic and supportive; it raised funds on their behalf and provided strong testimonials vouching for the goodness and trustworthiness of the baby's parents. Friends, employees, and neighbors all spoke well of them. They were poor, but they were decent and hardworking. He was a construction worker in his 30s, and she was a department store clerk, and a student at a community college.

Alice could not understand why their son had not been returned to them after so long. It had been over three weeks. How could they think that her husband would hurt his own baby deliberately? Or why, being that it was an accident, could they not get him back? Alice was angry and militant. Andrew was paranoid, guilt ridden, and despondent. They often argued.

One evening, after Andrew met with their court-appointed lawyer, they had a big row. The judge had just postponed a court hearing to rule on Andrew's guilt or innocence for three more weeks. The postponement was like a sentence to live in limbo for three more weeks. Alice was livid. She demanded to know why. Andrew told her that the lawyer surmised that perhaps the judge needed more time.

"Good grief! It's been over a month, and he still wants more time?" Alice protested. "How much longer does he need?"

"I don't know," replied Andrew sheepishly. "I just don't know. We'll just have to wait. The three weeks will go by fast."

"Andrew, three weeks in hell do not go by fast! That will be three more weeks before we can bring our baby home."

At the sound of that, Andrew realized that Alice did not understand the nature of their situation and proceeded to enlighten her.

"Whoa there! Hold your horses. I think there is a great misunderstanding here. You seem to think that the hearing in three weeks is to give us our baby back. But you are wrong. Don't confuse the two things: the dropping of charges against me and getting our baby back. They are two separate things. They can clear me of charges tomorrow, but still keep Tony in the foster home indefinitely."

"But why?" she demanded. "That's not fair! What reason could they possibly have for keeping him once you have been cleared of any abuse charges?"

That evening they talked and argued late into the night. There were so many things that made no sense to her. What would have happened if she and her husband had been divorced and living apart at the time of the accident? Assuming the accident had occurred in his apartment, would they still have taken the baby away from her? Why? Where would be the justice in that? She felt that the courts were taking it out on her unjustly as they tried to punish Andrew. She also felt that she could provide better care for her baby than he was getting at Mildred's. As far as she was concerned, the baby belonged with her, and it was high time they returned him to her. She also tended to minimize the extent of the baby's injuries.

Andrew was more realistic. He had a different perspective because he had dealt directly with the lawyers, doctors and case workers. The child abuse charge was not the major issue anymore, even though there was a letter from a doctor, an expert on these cases, who had testified that the injuries appeared to have been inflicted deliberately and maliciously. Andrew admitted having shaken the baby and causing the damage. But he didn't mean to. It was not abuse. Their lawyer assured them not to be concerned too much about the expert's letter because, after all, he had expressed his opinion from far away, over the phone, without even examining the baby personally, or the father for that matter.

The main concern of the state now was the care of the baby. Baby Tony had been in and out of the hospital for various reasons, the gravest one to drain fluid from his brain. He needed daily physical therapy because he had motor deficiencies. His hearing and vision could have been impaired, but it was too early to determine the extent. The question was whether the Stewarts could provide the necessary care for the baby. Andrew had to clobber Alice with these issues till she faced them honestly and realistically. She was part of the problem. She was too Pollyannaish about the baby's future. She had not come to grips with the possibility that Tony might be wheelchair bound for the rest of his life; that he might be retarded and perhaps even deaf or blind. While her mind could accept the worst scenario, her heart resisted it and denied it.

It was a painful evening for both, especially for Alice. The night grew long, and after they went to bed it grew even longer when in the silence of darkness their minds continued to be engaged in the subject independently. Andrew finally fell asleep around three in the morning; Alice tossed in bed until 4:30 a.m. battered by a storm of thoughts that would deny her calm. The following day they both went about their chores without missing a beat, despite the shortness of sleep. Alice listened to the 11 o'clock news. The Terri Schiavo case was still at the top of the news. This time Alice heard it through. The catharsis of the night before had helped her cope with that dark awful reality. By noon, she was alone with her baby again.

"Well, hellooo, my Love! You glad to see Mommy? No, you are not! You are a sleepy baby today. That's okay. You go right on and sleep. Mommy will hum you a lullaby. Hmmm, hmmmm, hmmmm." She hummed a tune to him, and after a few minutes of silence she resumed talking to him.

"Oh, Sweetheart, I wish so deeply—more than ever—that you could learn to say 'Mama.' It would mean so much to me, and it would prove once and for all that you could hear, that you could learn and remember, that you could make associations, that you could recognize your Mommy, and that you could get your little vocal cords in gear to form a word. Oh, that one little word would mean so much! It would speak volumes of promise, of wonderful things to come. If I could give everything I possess, even my life, in exchange for you saying that word, I would do it! It would mean that much to me because it would mean you are going to be all right. Everything I own is a small price to pay for the ransom of all your senses. I mean that."

Alice sobbed a little as she cradled him in her arms. Then a disturbing thought visited her mind. As she looked at her baby, she sensed he had become the embodiment of her conscience, and he wanted to say something for the record. "But Mom, what if I can't see, or hear? What if I can't think like others? What then?" And she had to respond to his questions.

Her first response was denial. "No, no, that cannot be. I'll fight it to the gates of hell."

The baby persisted. "Please, Mom. This is me asking you. Please don't dismiss it. Face it. Tell me what you would do if the worst came to pass. I need to know how you will handle it."

Alice broke down in sobs. When she collected herself again, she responded to the baby's query. "Aah, yes. What if it were true... what if the doctors' fears came to pass... I don't think they will... but yes, what if you could not hear me, what if you could not see me—Oh, dear God!—I don't know, oh Darling...What then?" Alice sobbed again as she cradled her baby, clutching him. Then after several minutes, she dried her tears and continued bravely with resolve.

"Well, my Sweetie, all these what-ifs are hard to take. But there is one thing I must tell you and you must believe it. It's very important. Even in the worst of cases you must know that I will still love you. I'll love you no matter what! Don't you ever forget it! And another thing, I'll never give up fighting for you. I will search high and low for cures, for specialists, for new treatments. I won't give up. But if, after trying out all leads and hopes, if in the end that is not to be, then so be it. I will be by your side. I will learn what I need to learn—Braille, Morse code or whatever—but I will communicate with you. Even then, one way or another, whether by tapping on your little hands or what-have-you, I will try to bring the world to you, seeking for those ways, those connecting lines, those means to reach you. That will be my quest.

"If Helen Keller, who was deaf, mute and blind, could overcome her incredible handicaps and learn to read, to write, to finish college and become world famous, I'll keep the faith and aim for no less. We will aim for the sky; we will grow wings, and we'll learn to fly. I promise you. Nothing will bind you to ignorance and keep you from knowledge. We will aim high.

"Ah, and one more thing, my Sweet, as with every other child, our first word will still be 'Mama.' The day when you first say it to me in whichever way you can, whether you touch my face with your little hand, or whether you lip-sync it, whichever way you do it, I will rejoice and you will read a smile from me, a smile with tears of joy. That one word, that little drop of vocabulary will open the floodgates of your learning. You will absorb the world one word at a time from then on. I promise."

A final note. Baby Tony lived to the age of three. A year later, his parents divorced.

# WORDS ALSO DIE

Words die without obituary. The train of language leaves the station for the future, but the word is not on it. After several years, lexicographers notice their absence and begin making dismissing remarks, calling them rare, obsolete or archaic. Eventually a heap of centuries buries the words, but their skeletons remain in old folios in the garb of their ancient calligraphy, without meaningful resonance anymore.

But long before words disappear from the language, words first die in the brain of their human hosts. So, it is in the human brain that we must go to find the beginning of the demise of words. For the human brain is everything to a word. It is an incubator; it is maternity ward; it is playground and school; it is workplace, battlefield and, ultimately, it is cemetery as well.

Where exactly in the human brain do we find words? And what form do they take there? Scientists would have their own approaches to these questions and, no doubt, they would involve neurology—although, from what I understand, they are still in the dark ages in this regard. I prefer a humanistic approach.

I envision words in human form and I picture vocabulary as concentrations of words, like cities, like villages and communities within the brain. Some words have class and status. Some words are well-off while others are poor; some are healthy while others infirm; some are secure while others live in peril. The world of words is pretty much like ours. It is a dynamic world in flux battered by waves of change that come and go and turn some words from economically secure to homeless paupers, from healthy to ill, from popular to pariahs. In the boonies of the brain some words bounce with the wind like tumbleweed.

Incredibly, there are also sinister forces at work, like plagues of prejudice, racism and bigotry that result in the death of entire communities of words, pretty much like ethnic cleansing. The source of these maladies invariably traces back to the human host. A poison in his blood pollutes the ambience, making that brain hostile to certain words. The following is an account of how this happens.

### *The Story of Undre.*

Although she was a word, do not picture her as so many letters. Picture her, instead, as an attractive young woman in her late twenties whom friends and neighbors had affectionately nicknamed Undre because her real name was long and unbecoming, and she did not want to be burdened with dragging its cross.

She lived in an area of the brain that had been condemned for redevelopment, where all her friends and neighbor were pariahs, social rejects, words that had fallen through the cracks and had outlived their usefulness. It was a shantytown near a dumping ground in the outer fringes of a slum, out of the reach of transportation, sewerage, telephones, or electric power. In this hardscrabble world the homeless fashioned their domiciles out of whatever served as shelter—a shed, a crate, a railroad car, a bus.

Her own abode happened to be a cramped, old, rusty VW van; half buried in the dirt. Now the demolition squads had been summoned, the bulldozers were coming, and the days of the shantytown were numbered. They were making space for new vocabulary.

For months, Undre had managed to eke out her existence on diminishing remnants of trash, while all around many of her peers were dying from the malnourishment meted out by willful neglect. None of them understood the causes of their bad times, or how they had drifted into such a dystopian state. They suspected it could be genocide but dismissed the possibility as too frightful. In any case, they could not understand why. Was it deliberate or was it unintended? If it was deliberate, what offense had they committed? What made them so damnable? They searched for their faults but could find nothing that warranted such hatred. They didn't even know who their enemy was. They were collateral damage in a war between unknown enemies; they were at the wrong place at a bad time. Perhaps it was all a misunderstanding. Perhaps the government was not aware of their plight. Perhaps they were going through a transitional period before being relocated to better quarters. Perhaps there was a simple explanation for everything.

Everyone looked up to Undre who was still strong and in better shape than the others to get answers. So, she volunteered to go to City Hall to get to the bottom of their story once and for all. As she left, she prayed silently that it was a misunderstanding or unawareness of their plight. If it was, she was ready to forgive and forget. How nice that would be. But if it was no mistake, if it was deliberate, if it was genocide, oh God, she didn't know what she would do. She didn't have the energy to fight anymore. What could she do then? Of this, she was sure. She would tell her people the truth, no matter what the truth was. If it was no mistake, if it was deliberate, if they were being deliberately exterminated, she would tell them so and she would tell them why. Their only consolation would be the knowledge of their fate, the reason for the hatred, the origin of their curse, the cause of their misfortune.

They knew they had one element in common. They were all words from Economics. But none of them could imagine why that should be a crime or cause for extermination. What is so offensive about that? Undre had her own suspicions. She thought ignorance and stupidity were involved. Her own name was a good example. She was christened *underemployment,* a name that confused people. It was technical, alien and esoteric. What reason, other than this, could explain the fact that she was among the outcasts, while her cousin, *unemployment*, lived in town and was well off? Undre suspected that people considered her a highfaluting synonym for unemployment and, as such, superfluous.

It was almost dark by the time Undre returned to her junkyard from City Hall. In the twilight, the desolation and misery of her neighborhood was ever more depressing. Its pauper cemetery was not only lugubrious, but pitiable for its penurious tombstones fashioned out of cardboard, and its crosses formed out of sticks and twigs.She went past her van to see her neighbor Empi, short for MPC (marginal propensity to consume). His abode was a loosely hung tarpaulin tent next to her van. She found him sprawled on a bench outside his tent fast asleep.

"Wake up Empi" she said as she shook him gently.

"Oh, hi, Undre. What's up? You've been gone for ages."

"Yes, I know. I can't get rides anymore and I walk slowly. Gone are the days when we had the money for bus fares. Remember the times when they needed us so badly that they sent a taxi to get us, and we rode in style to make an appearance at the Merriam Webster or at the glossary of an economic pamphlet? Remember the times when they had us perform on the pages of a textbook? I made a turn or two and danced a few ballet steps on those pages."

"Ah yes, that was our golden age. But you must be tired. Why don't you just relax now? You deserve a rest."

"Well, I'll tell you this much now. I did talk to a city functionary, a councilman, or something. He was very nice, and I finally got what I went for. I have the answers to all our questions. But maybe you are right. Let me catch my breath first. Meanwhile, you tell me what's happened here while I was away."

"Plenty," replied Empi. "The place is getting noisier. They brought in one of those big cranes with a grappler that hoists the metal junk and dumps it into a compactor. They just quit for the day about an hour ago, but they'll be back tomorrow. Oh, and we have two more bodies to bury today. This time it's the Non-Discretionary-Fiscal-Policy-Stabilizers. The both of them."

"Poor dears!"

"I must confess, Undre, I never knew what they stood for. Did you?"

"Yes, I did. How sad. Even insects have friendlier names than they. One of them stood for unemployment compensation. The other for the progressive income tax. What made them non-discretionary? And what made them fiscally stabilizing?

Both have stabilizing features built into them. These features are automatic—as opposed to deliberate or discretionary. Congress doesn't have to take specific "discretionary" fiscal action to correct the swings of the business cycle.

So, suppose the economy is beginning to overheat. Employment is growing and prices are rising. In this situation, the federal government should lower spending. And bingo, unemployment compensation automatically decreases because the government has fewer and fewer unemployed people to compensate. In this situation you also want to temper private spending. And, again bingo, the progressive income tax sees to it that people pay more taxes automatically. As they do, they have less disposable income to spend.

It also works in the other direction. If the economy is entering a slump and becoming sluggish, then it would make sense to stimulate spending. In this case, unemployment begins to increase, but as it does unemployment compensation automatically triggers in, alleviating the situation. Also, in this situation the progressive income tax system automatically decreases tax collections, thus increasing disposable income and spending. For all that they do, these features are like guardian agents to the economy; they should have coined seraphic names for them instead of the gobbledygook jargon."

"Thanks for the explanation, Undre. It's so sad. They died in their sleep. I found them next to each other in a half embrace with no pulse. Their bodies were already cold and tough, as if rigor mortis had set in some time ago."

"Shish, you can say that again," said Undre. "Rigor mortis started for them at birth. They were half-dead from the first day they came here. I remember when they came in. They were brought here like preemies, deformed and only half alive. They had a bad life from the start. Nobody knew who begot them; nobody ever understood what they were about. Nobody wanted what they had to offer. They were brought into this world to be scorned."

"Well, we don't need to do anything about them tonight. I have informed everybody about their passing. I don't think anyone is in the mood for services of any kind. This sort of thing is becoming commonplace. People seem to take death with a shrug now."

Both were aware that death was taking a greater toll on the living with each passing day. The funeral services were draining them for all the digging and burying.

"All this is getting to be too much with me," said Undre. "Burials are getting to be a pain. They are a big waste now. We ought to think of something else to do with the dead bodies."

"I agree completely, but do you have something in mind?"

"Maybe we just drag them to the old, dilapidated school bus and sit them there. Let them ride into the sunset like that."

"But that's just a few yards from here! What would you do when they start to decompose and smell bad?"

"Good point. I hadn't thought of that."

"Here is a better idea," said Empi. "What if we just took them a few yards further and threw them over the cliff? I don't think we'd have a problem with the smell then."

"Maybe not, but good heavens, has it come to that already? It's one thing to leave them side-by-side, with some dignity, and let nature take her course. It's quite another to dump them like sacks of trash over a cliff. Ugh, I don't like that."

Empi said nothing. Dumping them didn't bother him at all. They thought about the situation silently.

"You know, Undre, I think animals—cats especially—could teach us a thing or two."

"How is that?"

"They seem to know when death is near, and they make themselves scarce and seek a secluded place to wait for death out of the range of the living. They just vanish."

"That would be good. But we are not cats."

"Also, I've been thinking, Undre. Do you realize that one of us might die before the other? If I'd die first, I sure don't want to be a burden to you. And chances are I will go before you. I've been thinking about moving my tent up to the edge of the cliff so that when the time comes all you have to do is roll me over the edge with a minimum of effort. I wouldn't hold it against you if you did that. Could you do that for me?"

"Oh, I don't know Empi. What if I were to die first? But really, right now I would rather not talk about this anymore. We have had enough morbidity for one day. Let's change the subject for now. Want me to tell you what I found out in town today?"

"Oh yes, by all means, I've been waiting all day to know."

Undre began. "Everything makes sense now. I've learned how all this came to pass, why we are here in this forsaken place, as if marooned in a desolate planet. All we can do is to look at the stars and see what might have been. Look at them, Empi. What do you see?"

"In the stars?"

"Yes, in those distant worlds full of promise, some of which sustain intellectual life and are hospitable to words of our ilk. I see paradise in many of them—paradise which could have been ours. Look at them glitter as if inviting us, as if saying: you are welcome to live here, if you could just get here somehow. But they are so far, so out of reach. Instead, we are marooned here, beyond rescue."

Empi was scratching his head with a befuddled look. "You kind of lost me, Undre. I thought you started to tell me what you learned today, but then got sidetracked about the stars."

She smiled at him. "Sorry about that. I'll come to that. The stars are a perfect metaphor for our situation, Empi. They are the shining promise of the unreachable, what could have been: rich, happy, exuberant wonderful life whose fragrance I can almost smell across the cosmos. But being too distant, they serve only as a reminder of what cannot be.

"Those stars you see up there are minds, Empi; they are other people's human brains. Many of them have room for the likes of you and me, unlike the brain we occupy, unlike this desolate wasteland we inhabit. But let me get back to earth and tell you about today. You will see what I mean.

"At first, I got some run around at City Hall. They thought I was a beggar out to panhandle. They avoided me like the plague. But then I found a kind-hearted civil servant who took pity on me and took me aside to give me a hearing. That was all I asked for. By then I was about to burst into tears out of sheer frustration. He confessed that he did not know what *underemployment*

meant. He confirmed what I suspected. He thought I was an esoteric synonym for *unemployment* and that people preferred *unemployment* because it was simple and clear. If that was the cause
of my problem, there was nothing he could do. People are fickle
and it is just too bad if they considered me superfluous.

"I could have just killed him. So, I lectured him. I told him
he was wrong about that. In the first place, I am not a synonym.
There is an important difference. Underemployed doesn't mean
you are unemployed. In fact, quite to the contrary, when you are
underemployed you have a job, but it is a stupid wasteful job that
doesn't take advantage of your potential. A surgeon who is working as a nurse would be underemployed, a yardman who has to
cut the grass manually on his knees with shears because he is
not given a lawn mower would be underemployed. Perhaps, *mis-
employed* would have been a better term. He got the idea. He understood the distinction and he apologized. That's when he really
started listening to me. I also made it clear that I was not there
on a strictly personal mission. There were others like you and
me—many, many more. All of us had one thing in common. We
were all words from economic jargon. Why should that be the
cause of the cruelty we've experienced for months now?

"That really got his attention. He went and got a big ledger and
a couple of other books, and he started looking in earnest. As he
looked, I could tell from his expression that the news was bad.
It took him quite a while to get the big picture. Then, finally, he
closed the books and told me the long story.

"He began by saying that the whole of Economics was anath-
ema to our host brain. It was as undesirable as German, if not
more so. I was lost by all that, so I begged him to cut out the mum-
ble-jumble and let me have it plain and straight. What does Economics have to do with German?

"Then he gave me the background, telling me that the pro-
prietor of this gray matter is a young woman, and she happens

to hate Economics and German. For good reason. We are talking about a young college coed who last year was infatuated with the foreign instructor of her Economics class. Everything was wunderbar, at first. Then she learned that the love of her life was engaged to marry someone at the end of the semester and, of course, everything went sour from that point. Our co-ed had totally misunderstood his blandishments, his kindness and playfulness with her. She felt so humiliated.

"It didn't take me long to figure out that the foreign instructor was German. A year ago, about this time, words in German or Economics were the darlings of this mind. Now this brain has gone to other interests. She is a cheerleader, and she is going to major in P.E. To her, Economics is such a bad episode in her life that she'd just as soon forget it all. It gives her nausea every time she thinks about it. To add insult to injury, she barely passed the course. She squeaked by with a C-, so she'll never have to take another Economics course for as long as she lives. She has given orders to delete all economic terms from these premises, especially all those words that she considers so, so dumb. Interestingly, this explains why my cousin, Unemployment, is alive and well, living in town with full services as a respected citizen. She is not esoteric as we are. She is an ordinary everyday word which people use daily.

"I thanked the man for his troubles and left. Do you get the picture now? Can you see how the stars represent other people's minds to me? I know that some of them could be the minds of graduate students of Economics. Some might even be professors of Economics, or Nobel laureates. Can you imagine what it would be like to live in one of those brains? We'd live in the lap of luxury. Well, Empi, that's the story of our sad circumstance."

"I get the picture, Undre. We are doomed. But now it's getting late. It's been a long day. Let's get some sleep."

They went their ways to their respective quarters. The next day when they met again, they discovered more bad news. There were more bodies waiting to be disposed of. Overnight two more had died: TIM, the Tax Incentive Multiplier guy, and LR, the erstwhile bubbly Liquidity Ratio. In his day he was bouncy, happy, friendly and foppish; always dressed in colorful Hawaiian outfits and people nicknamed him Horatio, the Liquidity Ratio.

Undre broke into sobs. "Oh, Empi what are we going to do?"

"Nothing," said Empi firmly. "We are going to do nothing about them. I don't have the energy, and I don't care anymore."

"What about us? What are we going to do about us?

He hugged her and patted her, trying to console her.

"I don't know about you, Undre. I don't know what you want to do, but I know what I want. I would like to ask a favor of you, but I am afraid to ask."

"Oh no, please, don't be afraid. You've been so good to me. I'll do anything for you. What is it?"

"I want you to help me get where I want to go. I don't think I can make it on my own."

"To the edge of the cliff?" Undre asked.

"No, I am past that. That's not good enough. I am tired of this useless waiting. I'm tired of seeing the flame of my spent candle flicker hopelessly in this wasteland, and all for what? I want to snuff it out. Now that I know the hopelessness of our situation, I can't see a reason not to."

"Oh dear, dear Empi. I do understand. I know exactly what you mean. Don't hesitate to ask me. Just tell me where you want to go and I'll take you there, no matter where."

"I want you to help me walk the distance to the terminator, over to the place where the bulldozers and the great compactor-shredder pick up the junk and break it and smash it to smithereens. When we get there, just leave me in any old truck we can find. That's what I want. Could you do that for me, Undre?

I hate to ask you to do such a thing. But I don't have the strength to get there on my own and I don't want to just sit and wait here anymore. Waiting is for those who harbor hope, and I have none anymore."

He had a lot pent up within him and wanted to get it off his chest.

"For too long I've juggled faith and hope, always keeping one up on the air, trying to maintain my sanity. But I have nothing to hope for anymore. The game is over. This place is no better than those squalid dungeons in medieval castles—oubliettes I think they called them—where they used to dump people, throwing away the key, and forgetting about them. I have often wondered what made people do that. Was it incompetence to kill, or was it perversity, pleasure in the cruel sport of making people die slowly? Well, I am tired of playing this waiting game. I can no longer continue to exist just to accommodate the world's perversity or its inefficiency at killing. That is why I must go to the shredder."

Undre said little. She just uttered the necessary words to let him know that she was listening and that she cared. "Yes. Yes," she said. "I know. I know."

"Well then, what are we waiting for?" asked Empi. "I am ready to go now. I want this to be the last day of my life."

They got underway, talking as they walked, stopping to rest at times.

"Do you know what pains me the most?" Empi asked as he called for a rest. He looked into her eyes glazed by a mist of sadness. "Now I understand what you meant when you said the stars were our unreachable havens."

Talking had become more difficult. The noise of the junkyard was louder as they approached their destination, and the cacophony of destruction drowned out all other sounds. The thump and clatter, the screech of metal grinding, the rumble of steel cables dragging, and the roar of cranes, and bulldozers filled the air with the sounds of a war zone and voice communication became inaudible and difficult. Then at last they were amid it all and it was frightening and exhilarating. Empi beamed with wonder as he looked at the giant machinery around him. He was like a child at a state fair, fascinated by the rides.

"Where's a good place to embark?" he asked her, as they came to several big pieces of junk that were in line for the grappler.

"I don't know—wherever you want. It's your call, Empi."

"Okay, let's try that," he said as he pointed to a garish, red and yellow tourist trolley with long rows of seats, and a tattered canvas roof. That trolley was about fourth or fifth in line to be picked up and would give them a little time to say goodbye. He was leaning on her in earnest by now. He needed her support.

When they reached the trolley, she seated him on the edge of one of the rows of seats and stood outside beside him, waiting, saying nothing, but holding one of his hands as they watched the heavy machinery at work, lifting, crushing and mangling. Then, after a few minutes, she motioned him to scoot over; she would sit with him for a while. They sat together quietly exchanging glances, smiling from time to time, until a grappler with huge iron talons descended and encircled the vehicle and began to shake it loose from the ground. Empi then shouted: "Oh, Undre, you've got to jump now. You can't stay here! You've got to go."

But she remained seated beside him, embracing him tightly with one of her arms around his shoulders. As he pleaded with her, she brought her index finger to her lips, making a sign saying: "Hush." He pleaded again with a plaintive facial expression, but she nodded her head with resolve, asserting firmly that she would not be jumping off. When the crane hurled them up in the air, there were tears of joy in their eyes.

The crane lifted them high up in the air with a big swing. The exhilaration was so vivid they could hear their hearts sing. Un-

dre's face was radiant with joy, her eyes all aglow, yipping exuber-
antly: "Whee! Whee! Look at us go!"

# LAPIDARY WORDS

---

They argued heatedly and often, mother and offspring. This time it was over cremation versus burial; the old lady extolling the virtues of burial, insisting that that was what she wanted; the sons and daughters expatiating on the advantages of cremation, disparaging against burial. They noted that most of their relatives had been cremated recently.

"How disgusting, Mother, to have your remains rotting in a casket with worms feasting on your spoiling flesh. How can you possibly endure the thought of that?" asked Marta, the pediatrician and oldest daughter.

"That's the way of the Lord. That's the way the church would have us turn into dust," said Señora Rosa.

"Ah, but you are wrong, Mom," corrected Alicia, the accountant, and youngest daughter. "The church has changed its stand on that. The Pope doesn't object to cremation anymore. Catholics choose it often now."

"Well, maybe so, but I am not other people. And I want to be buried."

Marco the host and second oldest had his go at the issue. "You realize, Mother, that this discussion is a bit silly because when you are dead, we can cremate you and you won't feel a thing. What difference does it make after you are dead?"

"*Carajo!* (Damn it!) You are so dumb sometimes, Marco. Of course it won't matter then. That's why we are having this discussion now," said the mother, as she banged her cane in anger.

Everybody roared laughing. "Man, she got you," Alice told Marco, rubbing it in. He shrugged his shoulders. Pepe, the third child in Public Relations, intervened, trying to advance the issue to the next stage.

"Okay Mom, you win. If burial is what you want, that's what you'll have. But tell us where. Is it Miami? Atlanta? Los Angeles? St Louis? Or Guayaquil?"

At the sound of the last city, she shrieked. "Ay, no! I don't want to be buried in Ecuador. What the devil made you bring that up? I got nothing there. No, no! Dios Santo, not there!"

Pepe apologized instantly. "Sorry about that," he said, taking back the suggestion.

"Absolutely, not in Guayaquil," the old lady ranted on. "What the devil is the matter with you? Why would you even bring that up? I haven't been there in fifty years. You are just trying to provoke me and get me mad. Hell, no, I don't want to go back there, dead or alive! I was from a small town in Manabí Province. I went to Guayaquil in my teens, and I always hated it."

"Go hide somewhere or she'll never stop," Alice told Pepe. "You've got her wound up now."

"All right already, Mom. We've heard you loud and clear. Guayaquil is off the map, off the face of the earth for you. We will never bring it up again. Forget about it. But change gears and tell us where you want to be buried. We need to know, you know."

"Yeah, Mom. Please think about another place and tell us, "Said Marta.

The old lady thought for a moment then she said, "I don't know. I don't care."

"Gee! That helps a lot, Mom," said Alicia, sarcastically, switching back to English. In that household they went rapidly from English to Spanish, depending on who was talking to whom. From sibling to sibling, it was always English, never Spanish. From mother to children and from children to mother, it was always Spanish, never English.

Pepe slipped back in from behind Señora Rosa's chair. "Okay, Mom, I got another city that I am going to risk asking you about. What about where I live, Los Angeles?"

"No, no. Not there. You come up with the most outlandish places. I've never even been there, and I am not going to go there dead," said Rosa.

The sons and daughters looked at each other as if a new game were in play, one that had just been invented, one in which each of the children would ask her about his or her city. Alicia took the next turn and asked about being buried in her city.

"What about Miami, Mom? Would you like to be buried there?"

The mother mulled it over briefly, and then she made a face of such disgust, as if she had gotten whiff of something rotten. She shook her head from side to side with her face wrinkled in a moue of displeasure as if she had bitten into bitter lime. Alicia then stepped aside as she yielded the floor with a gesture of defeat to the next city. Looking at Marta she said: "Go ahead, St. Louis."

Marta moved closer to her mother, but before she could even ask, Senora Rosa put it down, saying: "I don't want Miami or St. Louis. No, Sir, neither one."

Everyone looked at Marco, and Marco taking his cue from the stares, sprang to his feet and approached his mother, saying: "Well, I guess the ball is in my court. I guess it will have to be here in Atlanta."

The sons and daughters waited anxiously for their mother's reply. She was in a cul-de-sac, with nothing else but Atlanta now. But to everyone's amazement, she refused Atlanta also.

"No, I don't think so," said Señora Rosa. "Not Atlanta. No way!"

"Hey, where do we go from here?" asked Marta.

"I'm lost. This is hopeless," said Marco.

"Does she know what she wants?" asked Alicia.

"Okay, Mom, there are rules to this game," began Pepe. "You can't just leave us hanging in limbo like that. You say you don't want to be cremated. Fine. But you don't want to be buried anywhere either. That can't be. Help us out a little here. We assumed you would want to be buried in one of the cities where we live."

"Well, you assumed wrong," said Rosa.

"What do you want then?"

"She doesn't want to die," said Marco.

"No, I don't want to be buried in any of your cities. Who knows how long you'll live where you are now. You move too much. In a couple of years, you'll go who knows where and then I'll be left abandoned there. What's the point of that? It's not like in olden days when families lived together and remained together in one place, even after death. The modern world has gone to the dogs."

Pepe picked up on that saying: "Well, you are coming around to our side, Mom. You are making a great argument for cremation. Did you know that? You are pointing to the dynamics of the modern world, to its fluid and moving nature. There is nothing that can be done about that. That's why you adjust to circumstance and cremation accommodates the new order of things."

"I don't like this liquid world, and I don't like its adjustments and alternatives to burial. I still want to be buried."

"*Mamá*! You can't just say you want to be buried and not say where. We can't bury you in thin air. You've got to pick your ground, and you have to tell us where that ground is. That's why we are having this conversation, remember? So, where is it going to be?" protested Marco.

The old lady said something that threw all her children for a flip. She actually named a place.

"I think I want to be buried in Bonaventure."

Everybody was dumbstruck by her reply. They could not believe that she had chosen a place, especially one where she had no family or friends anymore. Still incredulous, they all wanted corroboration.

"Bonaventure? The cemetery in Savannah?" asked Pepe.

"Yes, the Garden of Good and Evil..." added Marco, in reference to John Berendt's book.

"I don't know about your 'garden of good and evil.' I don't know what you are talking about. But you are all acting dumb as if you had forgotten the city that embraced us when we first came from Ecuador, where we lived happily for so many years, where the last two of you were born, where my memories are buried. What's the matter with you? What is so wrong about wanting to join my cherished memories? I have friends buried there."

The children all approved the choice enthusiastically and assured her that there was nothing wrong with it. Savannah was great.

"It's a beautiful choice," said Marta. "Buena Aventura es bellisimo, Mami."

"Actually, if you want to go by beauty, the one in Guayaquil is stunning, infinitely more elaborate and impressive," remarked Alicia aside.

"Shssh! Don't bring that up again," shushed Marta. "It is also spooky as hell. That's one of the things she didn't like about Guayaquil. She was freaked out by that cemetery."

"Well, the important thing is that we've settled the issue. That's that. Bonaventure it is," said Pepe. "We've accomplished a lot for one day."

"Not as much as you think. There are so many details to be settled yet. Who is going to contact Bonaventure and handle the details? All of us live too far from Savannah, except Marco. And then, what does she want? Does she want a mausoleum, or what?"

"I should hope not! Mausoleums are expensive."

"Calm down. Let's ask her. Let's see what she wants."

"Okay, Mom, we got your resting place nailed down. We are making progress. Now you need to help us with other arrangements. What else do you want?"

"I want to go to bed."

The sons and daughters laughed at her abruptness. The girls helped Señora Rosa to her bedroom where she changed clothes and got into bed. She wanted to watch her *telenovela* in Univision. The sons dispersed to join their wives and children watching TV and playing games in another room.

There was no further discussion on the matter until much later that evening after the daughters had put Doña Rosa to bed. Marco and Pepe were still in the living room and Marta broached the subject. "Okay, so what are we going to do about Bonaventure?"

She quickly learned that Marco was not going to make any moves about funeral arrangements. Left to his own devices, he would do nothing till the day she died, and if no arrangements had been made by then, he would argue for cremation once again. If he had to accept a burial, he would still argue for burial in Atlanta, not Savannah as agreed upon. Pepe was also inclined that way. Doña Rosa, who knew her boys, had predicted that. She had told her daughters in her bedroom that their brothers had no intention of honoring something they did not believe in. If it was left up to them, they would win cremation by default, by doing nothing.

When Marta and Alicia confirmed their mother's suspicion, the sisters were furious. "How could you be part to a promise, and then renege on it, just like that?" asked Marta with some indignation.

"Get this straight," Marco responded. "I didn't promise her anything. Pepe did. She knows I don't believe in cemeteries; she knows I don't go there for anybody. I've told her she can get her burial, but she can't prevent being forgotten—as most tombs in cemeteries are. At first, she may have a few visitors, but in less than ten years her tombstone will be overrun by weeds—if the cemetery still stands and they haven't passed a road through it. I've told her this and much more; I've expressed myself bluntly. Now if the rest of you want to bury her, I can't stop you. Go ahead. It's your project."

"Mom sure got your number, Marco," said Alice.

"Well, I'm not through," continued Marco. "I think one can pander too much to the whims of people on this matter. I want to tell you an anecdote that I would like to have you think about and give me your input. It is the story of a homeless man in his eighties who had no relatives. He lived on welfare, and during the last months of his life he went into a nursing home. His greatest possession was a black suit he kept in an old suitcase. He told the attendants repeatedly that he wanted to be buried wearing that suit. He said he needed it to make a good impression in the world beyond. He also took one of the orderlies into his confidence and told him that he had five ten-dollar bills in one of the pockets of his suit. He would let him keep $20 for himself if he would swear to leave the other $30 in the pocket so he could be buried with them. He also asked the orderly to keep quiet about this because other people would not understand. He explained that he needed the money in the afterlife for transportation—something about paying a ferryman. The orderly said 'sure, sure,' and humored him along.

"The orderly was fond of the old man and wanted to please him. But it was stupid to bury thirty dollars. After mulling it over, he reached a compromise. He would keep the spirit of the promise. He would bury $10 with the old man and keep the rest. This way his conscience wouldn't bother him.

"But on the day the old man died, while the orderly was dressing him, he discovered hidden pockets in the coat's lining. All in all, the stash amounted to $1,500. I have two questions for you all now. What do you think the orderly did? And what would you have done in his place?"

Alicia was the first to blurt out her answer, saying: "I think the orderly buried the man with $10 and kept the rest for himself. As for me, I would have kept the whole enchilada, but to save my conscience, I would have written him a check for $1,000 to be cashed in heaven."

Marco was relishing what he was hearing. "Hmm, very interesting . . . " he noted.

Marta spoke next. "It's not so important what I would have done," said Marta. "I probably would have turned in the money in its entirety to the nursing home authorities. But first I would have notified the press to keep everybody honest. What I find more interesting now is speculating on what you would have done, Marco. Shall I tell you what I think you would have done? I think you would have lectured that poor guy night and day, day after day, on the folly of wasting his money. You would have told him that there is no afterlife and to forget the ferryman. You would have tried to convince him on cremation. He would have regretted that he ever confided in you."

Marco responded immediately. "Ha, you think you know me, Sister, but not well enough. Believe it or not, I might not have bothered to change his mind if I thought there was no glimmer of intelligence there and if I thought that reasoning would have been wasted on him. In that case, I would have humored him along and done exactly what you said you would have done. I would not have taken a penny for myself, but I, too, would have broken my promise. I would not have buried any money."

All eyes were on Pepe. "Well, as for me, I also would have tried to assess how flexible his mind was. If he seemed receptive to reason, I would have tried to convince him that the ferryman was right here in this world, and that you were supposed to pay him before you died. I would have told him that the ferryman was none other than your fellow man. If he could not find a needy human being to whom he could give his money personally, then he could reach him through the usual intermediaries: the Red Cross, the Salvation Army, Goodwill, or the Church. That black suit of his could have been put to good use by giving it to a poor man who could have used it to attend a wedding, or a funeral. Ditto for the dough. Good deeds in this world would be rewarded in the next; that's how you would get the tokens to pay your way across the river Styx. But I want to get back to Mom's situation now. I think we can all see the parallels of this anecdote with Mom's case, except that she doesn't have a black dress or money to bury. She just wants to be buried, period. I want to make clear that I did promise her burial in Bonaventure, and that I'm not reneging. My problem is that I just don't think it is necessary to do anything about it tonight, or tomorrow. She is only 83 now, and she is not in that bad a shape as to require immediate action. She could easily live another ten years. So, what's the rush?"

"The rush is that she needs the assurance that her wishes will be respected while she's still alive," declared Alicia. "Furthermore, she feels she can't count on Marco, and she has her doubts about you, too, Pepe. So, it's up to the rest of us."

"Do you know how badly she wants this, Marco?" asked Marta. "I hadn't realized it myself until tonight when she asked us not to bother with Mother's Day presents, or birthday gifts, or Christmas presents for that matter. She asked us to wrap them all up into a single gift: a plot at Bonaventure. It may be irrational by your reckoning, but that is what she wants. So now let me ask you something, Marco. How would you feel if your wife and children were bent on burying you because they did not like cremation? Or what if you died first and it was mother who campaigned tooth and nail for you to be buried?"

"I would rise out of my coffin and kick ass."

"Aha! But that, in a way, is what Mom is doing!" said Alicia.

Marco spoke again. "Okay, let me set the record straight. This may come as a surprise to all of you. I don't give a damn how my body is disposed of after I am dead. I have indicated my preference for cremation, yes, but cremation is not a crusade with me. I don't worry about it. I don't waste a single minute thinking about it. Once I am dead, you are free to try to surprise me. Go ahead. See if I care."

There was calm for a few minutes. No one said a word, but each one was thinking about the funeral arrangements for their own death.

"You know," began Marta wistfully. "All this has made me examine my own preferences. I thought I was for cremation, but now I'm not so sure. You guys have never been to Glasco, the little town in Kansas where Charles, my husband, is from."

"No, but we've heard you talk a lot about it," said Alice. "I thought you said you didn't want to live there."

"Yes, I said that. But I think I would like to be buried there next to Charles."

"Really? Why?"

"Charles and I have visited the town several times in late May for Memorial Day. This is a homecoming period that coincides with the High School's alumni banquet when people come from all over the country to connect with their roots and see family and friends. Incredibly, some of the visitors are in their 80's. Without fail, everybody makes a pilgrimage to the cemetery. The cemetery is small and plain, but it has the warmth of a place for the living, being more like a park, serenely pleasant. There is nothing ornate or elaborate about it, and certainly nothing lugubrious and imposing. No big rows of live oaks as in Bonaventure, and nothing even hinting of a big necropolis, with lanes and passageways, bridges and overpasses connecting vaults like Guayaquil's. There are very few crucifixes, angels or statues. The marble goes strictly to the tombstones that bear the basic facts: name, date of birth, date of death, and the family relationships. There is only a single mausoleum. The adornment is mostly in evergreen topiary, and flowers. What is remarkable is the unity of families after death. There is a continuity of generations that goes back to the late 1800s when this part of Kansas was settled. Some of the people buried there were, in fact, homesteaders. The clusters of tombstones are like granite branches of family trees. Here lies the father, there lies the mother, and nearby their children. Not far are the parents of the parents. The basic record of this people's journey through this world is not just relegated to some archive, or written on the wind as it were, but planted on solid ground where it endures through decades. There is a sense of family gathering for the ages which seems quite appropriate, and I like that. Above all, the people there are definitely not forgotten.

"Charles does not care whether he is buried or cremated. But he does want a stone near his people, bearing his name and mine, and marking in durable marble our dates in history. We haven't thought about our children, but the presumption is that if we were there, perhaps they may want to join us someday. That would be nice."

"Isn't there any poetry anywhere?" asked Pepe.

"No, absolutely not! Remember, this is the Midwest, and people are terse and factual, not given to gushy and florid language on tombstones, in sharp contrast to what you see in Latin countries where the grief is vented freely, often in maudlin and saccharine verses. I think I have seen only two or three inscriptions, and they were all brief, and reserved."

"Oh, but I like the lapidary words," said Alicia expressing her disappointment over the thought of a laconic cemetery. "I always read the inscriptions when I visit cemeteries. I have seen some that are so touching that I wish I had taken notes and copied them. Some were mawkish, but some were simply sweet and brief, quite gripping—nothing cloy about them. One of my favorites was in a pet cemetery. The inscription read, simply: To Penny: She never knew she was a rabbit. I love that! So brief, so simple, and yet it says so much."

"Yes, I like that too," responded Marta. "But don't think for a minute that Midwesterners are incapable of expressing their sentiments poetically. On a recent business trip Charles brought back a newspaper from Salina, Kansas. There was an article about roadside memorials for people who had died on wrecks in the highways. One of these read: "If tears could build a stairway, and memories a lane / I would walk right up to heaven and bring you home again". Is that beautiful or what? I love the imagery and the power of those words."

The discussion on lapidary words continued late into the night with other family members joining them in the living room, but mostly as audience; the men mostly listening while Marta and Alicia compared notes on some of the most memorable tombs they had seen in cemeteries around the world, such as Père Lachaise in Paris, Bonaventure in Savannah, and La Recoleta in Buenos Aires. Then Marco, who had listened quietly while they carried on about the tomb of the medieval lovers Heloise and Abelard in Paris, and the Lovers of Teruel in Spain, finally spoke up and asked them to explain to him their curious fascination with cemeteries.

"Don't you find this sort of thing a little morbid? I never visit cemeteries when I travel—certainly not in cities with so much bounce as Paris and Buenos Aires. What a waste! Besides, cemeteries are creepy, and I find them downright disgusting—almost repugnant. So, I just don't get your necrophilic fascination with them."

The girls looked at each other as if asking who would have at him first. They were like horses champing at the bit to start. Alicia was the more irrepressible one and went first.

"It's the history, Stupid! It is the past lore, the culture of the place, the legends buried there. The dead are part of the grandeur of the city; they gave the city its pulse at one time. They may be silent and still, but their memory brings back to life a whole era. Do you know who is buried at Père Lachaise besides Heloise and Abelard? The list is enormous and not all French. Right off the bat I can name you Chopin, Gertrude Stein, Rossini, Oscar Wilde, Proust, Piaf, and Jim Morrison the rocker—he, by the way, is there because no other cemetery in the world would have him. And there are many, many more luminaries."

Marta, like a filly herself, could wait no longer, and jumped into the argument almost neighing.

"Absolutely! It is a cultural, historical experience. Take Chopin, for instance, who died in the mid-1800s, so long ago as to be a distant myth, somebody that legend made up. But when I stood in front of his tomb, near his bones, the experience was so overwhelming that, for me, he became human for the first time. So, this is where all those beautiful nocturnes and preludes came from! I now feel richer by the experience. It's the same with others. Visiting Père Lachaise is a discovering experience; the place is full of revelations. That fact alone makes the visit worthwhile.

"But there is something else, too," continued Marta. "Each of us has a unique and personal relationship with cemeteries. It is something that evolves as you grow up. You go from morbid fright of death in childhood to acceptance and equanimity as an adult. I'll never forget my earliest experiences with the cemetery in Guayaquil. I remember the main gate—an iron behemoth with heavy bars, solid and austere. There was writing in big letters over it, but it was inscrutable because it was in Latin, which added to the enigma and the spookiness of the place. I was so scared and mesmerized by those words that somehow, for whatever reason, I memorized them. I remember pronouncing the words to myself and hearing them reverberate like the incantation of an oracle booming inside my head. They made such an impression that, some forty years later, here I am with those words still etched in my mind:

*IN HOC NOVAE VITAE PORTA EST.*

As a child, I took those words personally. They spoke to me directly. And not knowing what they meant, I made up my own meaning and interpretation. I thought they admonished me to be a good kid; to be quiet if I went in; to be respectful, or else! There was a threat in those words that scared me senseless. It was not until many years later that I asked a priest to tell me once and for all what those words meant, and I finally dispelled their dark eerie mystery. The translation was:

*THIS IS THE GATE TO THE NEW LIFE.*

Marta was twelve years old, and Marco was eight when the family left Ecuador for the United States. Marco also had memories of that cemetery. He remembered being spooked by it and by those enigmatic words. He thought the words meant: ABANDON HOPE ALL YE WHO ENTER HERE. He had a friend who thought the words meant: I AM WAITING FOR YOU TO BE CARRIED PAST THIS GATE.

Marta continued. "Cemeteries no longer scare me. After all, I am 56 and I've made my peace with death. My thoughts now turn to other facets of death that are less macabre and more philosophical, such as the purpose of one's life, and one's accomplishments relative to that purpose. That's why Père Lachaise is so interesting. You go there knowing a lot about the people there; you go looking for them because you know what they made of themselves. They are not strangers; they are more like old acquaintances that are about to become closer to you."

The night was growing long. They had covered a lot of ground, and they had settled something important. Doña Rosa would be buried, and it would be in Bonaventure. Alicia, who was the only one that had driven to Atlanta, would detour through Savannah on her way back to Miami and make the preliminary inquiries. As they were about to break up, someone asked casually what their mother might want on her tombstone—if anything. Should they ask her? What might be her response? That elicited several wisecracks. Pepe suggested that as a hypochondriac she might want to vindicate herself and tell the world: I TOLD YOU I WAS SICK.

Alicia thought that she would want to have her walking stick beside the tombstone with words to this effect: "In life I used this cane for more than walking. Watch yourself!"

Marco thought that she would say: "I fought tooth and nail not to be cremated and I won. I am here because my children saw my way eventually and for that I am eterrrrrrrrrrrrnally grateful."

Marta did not think that she would want any words. It would suffice to have Dad's name beside her, and the name of all her children. No more and no less.

The following day, Señora Rosa was feeling perky and lively. She had had a good night's sleep, and she was basking in her victory, having won the battle of burial over cremation. She wanted to bury the subject. She did not want to think about death or funerals. When Marta brought up the issue of lapidary words, Doña Rosa thought the question was intrusive, inopportune, and impertinently premature.

"What brings that up? All my children are going nuts! Well, for your information, I am looking forward to quite a few more years of life and worrying about lapidary words is the farthest thing from my mind."

# WORD RESCUE

A word is lost in the recesses of your brain, trapped like a butterfly, fluttering and flapping her wings against the membranes of your consciousness, clawing at your nerves trying to get out, but it can't. It could be the name of a thing, or a person. You can picture the object or its nameless face; you can recall the smile; you can even hear the echo of its voice—but you can't think of the name. Who was that actress? Who was that politician? Curiosity intensifies beyond itching, reaching the threshold of madness. "What's in a Name?" Your sanity!

I will never forget the time the name of a song tormented me so. I was in Buenos Aires hearing and breathing tangos, Argentina's musical gift to the world. The night before I had gone to see a performance of GOTAN, a series of skits about tangos—half spoof, half serious, but all wonderful. Stories were woven together imaginatively and in such a way as to set up the situation of a tango, so that when the tango was sung, its lyrics fit the setup to perfection and brought laughter and applause. The show had a fantastic cast of singers and dancers, la crème de la crème: Susana Rinaldi, Raul Lavié, Carlos Copes and others. In the course of the evening, they sang part of a tango that I loved but had not heard in over 40 years. The lyrics (translated from Spanish) went like this:

*It's not so much that I regret having loved you*
*It's just that it saddens me how easily you forget*
*And your cheating breaks me up in tears.*

Like American country-western music, tango lyrics go for your soul and put it through a wringer. This tango had beautiful music, and dated back to the time of Carlos Gardel, Argentina's all-time idol, who recorded it before his death in 1935.

The lyrics and the melody of the tango flowed incessantly inside me, but its name frustrated me. I resolved to learn its name tomorrow. So, I hit the music stores on Calle Florida right after breakfast.

"I am here to buy several tango CDs," I announced to the young attendant who came to help me at the first music store I came to. It was a crisp sunny morning and Calle Florida, a well-known pedestrian throughfare in downtown Buenos Aires, was alive and buzzing. The attendant was delighted to have an eager customer ready to spend.

"I am looking for one tango in particular which I heard at the Gotan show last night. It is driving me crazy. I hope you have it."

"We shall see. I hope we do. What's the name of the tango?"

"That's the problem," I told him. "I can't remember the name."

An awkward silence followed. We were caught in the impasse of a pregnant moment. Now what do we do? He didn't know how he could help me without a name. He thought and hesitated and then awkwardly, slightly embarrassed, he ventured to ask me the only thing that made any sense. "Could you... like... give me a hint... by maybe singing a few lines?"

"Moi?" I shuddered. "Has it come to that?" Then, realizing that there was no other way, I took a deep breath and cleared my throat and intoned the above lyrics: "*No es que esté arrepentido*...It's not so much that I regret having loved you.

To my surprise, at that point he joined the singing. We both finished singing the first few lines in duo. I was delighted.

"Oh, great," I said excitedly, "so you do know it. What's the name?"

"Well, actually, er... I also know the lyrics, but not its name."

The unknown name was now trapped within two heads, desperately trying to come out. What a fix! Then the attendant assured me that one way or another he would find out.

"Don't worry. You just go on looking for other CDs while I go inside to find the name of this tango. Leave it to me."

I went about my business looking at CDs, adding several to my shopping cart, wondering if I should buy them there, or if I should hold off on that. Perhaps, if the attendant came back empty-handed, my best bet would be to go elsewhere and go through the same process.

Then, five minutes later I saw him coming from the back of the store waving a couple of CDs. "I have your tango," he said with great enthusiasm. "Here it is. It's La Mariposa. (The Butterfly)."

What a coincidence! That name which had been trapped in the cages of our brains like a butterfly was, indeed, a butterfly.

"I have a re-mastered version by Gardel himself, and also a newer version by Alberto Merino," the attendant told me. "So, you can have your pick. Would you like to hear them?"

"Most definitely!"

I liked both versions and bought them both, as well as several others to make his efforts worthwhile. But I was very curious to learn how he had determined the name. Did he have a special search engine on his computer?

"Please clear up something for me," I began. "How did you determine the name of the tango?"

"I phoned my father and told him neither of us knew the name."

"So?"

"He asked me to sing it, and I did. He is a big tango buff. I didn't even get to the end of the first line when he stopped my singing and blurted out: The Butterfly."

Mission accomplished, I took to the streets of Buenos Aires, humming the tango. It was as if I had opened a skylight to my cranium and now the cool crisp air of a sunshiny beautiful day flooded into my head. The cage that had imprisoned the tango had flung its doors wide open and now a beautiful butterfly hovered along above me like a halo, flitting in and out freely.

# WORDS AND
# REMEMBRANCE

I remember Monica Bruni for her love of language, her zeal and curiosity about words. As an Argentinean learning English, she found idiosyncrasies in English I never noticed. She put idiomatic expressions through a wringer. I can't help laughing as I remember her.

"Why," she asked, "if you can say: 'I am going to get some rest,' can you not say: 'I'm going to get a nap'? Why must you say, 'take a nap'?" She also questioned why you 'get' a respite, but you 'take' a break. I can just hear her say: "Ooooh, English is so capricious. It makes me crazy." Then she would ask: "You say capricious, no?"

"Yes, you could," I would respond hesitantly, "but it is a high-faluting word. People would say: English is 'difficult'."

Monica heaved at the sound of 'highfaluting' as a fisherman who just felt a tug on the line. "What was it you said? But wait, wait! Let me get my notebook before you tell me." Then she would run out looking for her little notebook where she recorded all the words of the day. When she returned, she asked: "Okay, how do you spell it? Flooting? Or fluting?"

"I don't think it's either one," I said, laughing at the predicament she had dragged me into. We looked it up and, lo and behold, we discovered that highfaluting is indivisible. *Faluting* by itself is meaningless; it does not exist. "I see what you mean about English being capricious," I commented wryly.

Another time she asked me: "Why do you say that someone acts like a Queen B. Why not Queen A, or Queen C?"

"It's not Queen B, Monica, but queen bee, like the little flying insect that makes honey."

"Ah, yes, la reina abeja. How could I have missed that?" Monica would say, reproaching herself as she took notes.

We met Monica during a business trip to Argentina in 2008. My husband, Al Wilkins, had to be in Buenos Aires for several days, and I tagged along. After concluding his business, we wanted to see more of the country. We went everywhere, but it was in Córdoba, Monica's province, that we met her. She was our guide through Córdoba City and environs, taking us to the nearby mountains and showing us places like the German community of General Belgrano, the Jesuit missions dating to the 16th century, and the quaint city of Alta Gracia where Che Guevara's house still stands and where the home in exile of Spanish composer Manuel de Falla is kept as a museum. Of course, Monica also took us to her city, Villa Maria, where we met her family. Monica's parents hosted us for dinner and were so kind that the visit forged a warm friendship between us and led to Monica's visit eight months later to our home in Savannah.

Monica beamed when I told her: "It is a shame that you have never been to an English-speaking country, Monica, loving the language as much as you do. You must come and visit us. We'd love to have you stay in our home."

From that moment Monica thought of nothing else. She arrived in Savannah in early February and left in mid-April. I had to remind her that February was a winter month here and to pack accordingly. It was summer in Argentina. We planned for Monica to audit classes at Armstrong State University so she would have a chance to meet people, to keep busy, and to gain an understanding of our educational system. Monica wanted to be an English teacher.

She caught Savannah at its best and saw the splendor of the azaleas when they bloom throughout in a spectacular explosion of colors. She saw the city go wild as a million visitors descended for St. Patrick's Day. We had heavenly weather throughout her stay. We took her to Atlanta, to Athens and places in between. Savannah was not what she had imagined. It seemed to be from another era and more English than American.

"That is no accident," I told her. "Savannah has worked hard to preserve its history and heritage. Some of the old buildings by the river date back to the 1700s, when the city was founded. The colonial part of town is full of relics, including the colonial cemetery, where some of the heroes that fought in the war of independence against the Brits are buried."

"Yes, but why the name Savannah?" Monica asked me with a puzzled expression. "I thought the city was named after a savanna, which is a treeless vast expanse of grass. But Savannah is covered by foliage, with parks every other block, with massive, gigantic trees that intertwine above the streets, forming arbors, tunnels of green everywhere. It is beautiful, yes. I love it. But it is not a savanna."

I shook my finger at her. "Ah, but you have only seen half of it. I need to show you the rest."

That same afternoon, I took her to the beach, twenty miles away, to the little resort town called Tybee and along the way we crossed the marshes, the grassy treeless plains that extend forever and are dotted by groves, small clusters of palms, resembling an oasis in an expanse of yellow grass. "How is that for a savanna?" I asked her.

"Oh, my goodness, it is a savanna," Monica exclaimed delighted.

She had also queried me about that other distinctive feature of coastal Georgia, asking me: "What is that clump of hairy-looking fibers that hang from the trees and look as if the trees had beards. What do you call it?"

"Spanish moss," I answered. She took notes.

She and I became very close. One day we were working in the kitchen preparing the food for a small party that evening. We were having a young man by the name of Vernon Parks, and a married couple, the Ortegas, who were both retired professors from Armstrong. Monica was making that staple in Argentinean cuisine, the beef empanada. Although we spoke in English, occasionally we would slip into Spanish to give me practice in that language. I asked Monica, "how do you say that someone is retired in Spanish? Is it retirado?"

"Yes, you could say that" answered Monica. "People would know, but the more common word is jubilado."

"I've never heard that! Anyway," I continued, "Bernardo Ortega used to teach Mathematics, and his wife, Claire, used to teach English. Both speak Spanish—Bernardo because he was originally from Colombia, and she by osmosis, I suppose. Tonight, I will trot out that strange word you just taught me. The young man, Vernon Parks, works for a software firm with my husband and adjuncts at Armstrong, teaching Information Technology. He is five years older than you, about 28. But he has an interest in Spanish because the firm is making inroads into Latin America."

Monica's hands were indisposed with empanada filling, and she could not access her notebook, so she had me write down two words I had just used: 'trot out,' and 'adjunct.' We had a delightful evening. The empanadas were a success, and I did use that word.

"So, how do you like being jubilado, Bernardo?"

"Ah, it is heaven on earth," he replied. "Life is a júbilo, a true jubilee."

It was then I realized that jubilado is derived from jubilee. Being retired is a state of jubilee. Of course, it has not gotten to that point in English. We just don't say: "He jubilated from his company last year." For Americans being retired and being in a state of jubilee are still two different things.

And yet, strangely enough, Monica saw no jubilee in retirement. To her, it meant simply not working.

"Why is that?" I asked her.

"I just don't have the same associations that you do. I don't picture jubilados as sporty old men, riding a red convertible with the top down, dressed in sports clothes and on their way to play tennis, or golf. The jubilados I picture are sad and tired old men who sit around playing checkers in the park; they sleep like babies on a rocking chair for hours. Life for them is nothing to jubilate about."

"That's very interesting," noted Al, who had been following the discussion. "Economic conditions in less affluent countries may have taken the jubilee out of the word by forcing people to work longer. They are worn out by the time they quit working and exist on a meagre pension. So, I can understand why Monica has a different picture."

Monica was nodding her head in agreement saying: "Yes, yes, yes!" Then, swinging her index finger for emphasis she added: "You have just hit the head with the nail."

People smiled, suppressing laughter. Monica blushed. She knew she had said something wrong. She looked at me puzzled. I told her, gently: "It's hit the nail on the head."

She took her notebook and wrote. Then she added, pensively: "You know... that expression has always bothered me. I do not understand it. What is it that is being hit? Isn't it the head of an issue? Aren't we hitting a problem on its head?"

"No, no," replied Al. "It's not the head of a problem. It is the nail's head that's being hit."

"The nail has a head?" Monica asked puzzled.

"Yes," said Claire. "You know, it's the flattened end of the nail, the end opposite the pointy part."

"Ah, so..." Monica said as she took notes. But it was obvious that the expression still frustrated her.

"It is stupid to me," she continued. "I can't see it. If that is the head involved, then where else would you hit the nail if not on the head? What else is there to hit? The nail doesn't have arms or legs!"

Now the room roared with laughter. A couple of us apologized and asked her not to take it personally. Her quirky logic had a point. Vernon was the first to see the problem.

"She is absolutely right, you know!" he said. "The expression 'hit the nail on the head' is incomplete. It needs a qualifier to make sense. What we mean to say is: 'hit the nail squarely on the head' because it's not what you hit, but how you hit it. You could hit the nail on the head, but obliquely, at an angle. Unfortunately, we've gotten in the habit of leaving out the critical word, 'squarely.'"

"Bravo. Bravissimo! Now that makes sense," said Monica thankfully while she scribbled frantically.


During the rest of the evening, we chatted about everything under the sun, but the subject of language resurfaced often because it hovered over Monica, like an aura. That notebook of hers had become an ever-present appendage of her persona. Sometimes she tried to be discreet about her notetaking, whispering, and writing her notes demurely without interrupting the conversation. Other times, if the word was important, she did not care if she stopped the world to catch it.

Although Monica's love of language was memorable, it was not her most impactful first impression. She was strikingly beautiful. She had long straight black hair that came down below her shoulders. Her face was thin and elongated; her forehead broad and radiant; and her eyebrows were richly endowed and neatly trimmed over vivacious smiling black eyes. Her body was svelte and lissome, about 5 feet 8 inches tall. In Argentina they call such brunette types, *Morochas*. She was the perfect specimen of one. Vernon had taken good note of all that and had figured that the best way to this beauty's heart would be through words.

After dinner I brought up the questions Monica had asked me for which I had had no answer, such as when to use 'get' as opposed to 'take.' Claire knew of no rule for that. She expressed her condolences about learning English. There are some things that you learn by just being here. "Welcome to the US, Monica."

"These verbs are awful," Monica said, and to prove it, she got her Harper Collins bilingual dictionary and showed everyone the entries for the verbs 'to get' and 'to take,' saying: "Behold these horrors."

The definitions ran for pages with so many qualifiers that changed the verbs into multi-headed monsters. We have get-up, get-down, get-in, get-out, get-around, get-by, get-at, get-after, get going, get behind, get-through, get-with, get-over and get-along. The verb to-take was just as bad. In many cases the meaning was intuitively obvious, but in others you just had to learn its special meaning as an entirely different word.

Monica moaned, as if overwhelmed by the phrasal verbs, pretending she was going to faint as she plumped down on the sofa. "Ah, what hope is there? How will I ever learn?"

Bernardo sat beside her, saying: "All languages have their barriers, Monica. They have their big mountain ranges which native speakers do not have to climb because they are born up there. But foreigners must scale up those mountains the hard way, step by step. So, take comfort in the fact that English speakers must scale our Spanish mountains also. If you looked up the Spanish verbs ser and estar in the same dictionary, you would find that they present formidable difficulties for Americans learning Spanish. To begin with, the verb ser is translated as 'to be' and estar is also 'to be.' What's the difference? Americans must work at it for years before they ever master the distinction which comes naturally to you. As if that were not enough, these verbs are highly irregular. Their conjugation is tortuous, helter-skelter, with no rhyme or reason. Pity the poor American students, trying to learn them. Yet there you are, prancing at the top of your Mt. Everest while Spanish learners are inching their way up to your heights. So, there is justice in the madness of Babel."

Monica stood up, smiling, humming, and turning, rubbing it in. Then she said, condescendingly: "Poor June, poor Al, poor Vernon, and poor Spanish language learners of the world. Tell me if you need me to throw you a rope."

"That's called gloating," I protested.

"Oh, my notebook, my notebook, where did I put it?" Monica said as she went looking for her notebook to record a new word.

While Monica searched for her notebook, I remarked about how treacherous languages are. "Yesterday Monica corrected my use of the word actualmente, which I thought was 'actually,' only to discover that something was awry."

Claire and Bernardo looked at each other as if they knew exactly in what sort of trap I had fallen. "*A faux ami!*" they said smiling.

"It happens when you are fooled, thinking that you know the meaning of a foreign word because it sounds so much like one in your own language."

Monica had re-entered the room and was taking notes frantically, fascinated by the concept of a faux ami.

"Did you get 'gloating' down, Monica?" Claire asked her good naturedly.

"Yes, yes. Please continue. I like this faux ami."

Claire continued. "In Spanish, the word 'actually' refers to something that is current, it is happening now. In English the word refers to something that is real and factual—as opposed to imagined or doubtful. When you used the word, you thought you were saying 'as a matter of fact,' but what Monica was hearing was 'at the present time.' There is a clear difference. So, suppose you were a natural blonde, but your hair was currently dyed red. And suppose someone asked you: What color is your hair? Your response could go like this:

"In the English sense of the word you would say: 'In fact, I'm really a blonde, although now my hair is red. In the Spanish sense you would say: Right now, I happen to be a redhead, but I'm naturally blonde."

"This is fascinating. I love it," beamed Monica. "Can you think of another example?"

"Yes, the classic example is a cliché by now. It is the word embarazada which sounds like the word 'embarrassed' in English. American women have used it thinking that it meant that. But it means being pregnant. Can you imagine the American woman's perplexity when she was complimented and asked when she was due?"

Then Monica thought of her own example, beaming eagerly, she said: "I know one, but it is maybe a little dirty. I don't know if I should tell it. Should I?"

Al responded emphatically, saying: "As head of this here household, I not only give you permission, but I hereby command you to tell it."

"The dirtier the better," added Bernardo.

"Well, this involves a misunderstanding between Spanish and French. All right?"

"Ah, good! This is beginning to get dirty already," said Bernardo.

"I am sure you have heard the French expression c'est la vie. It means: "that's life." It sounds very much like the Spanish clause se la vi, which means, er, how would you translate that, Bernardo?"

"I got to see her thing," he said.

"Thanks," she continued, already blushing. "One bright sunny day several people were standing around waiting for the bus. Among them were a Frenchman and a Spaniard. The Spaniard knew no French at all. Then along comes a gorgeous young lady. As she approaches, all eyes are on her. Suddenly, one of her heels breaks, and she falls flat on her back. The Frenchman goes to her rescue and gallantly lifts her up saying: 'Ah, c'est la vie, mademoi-selle.' Then the Spaniard, reproaching him, says: 'Well, I also got to see her thing, but I am not bragging.'"

The men applauded. Monica was red as a tomato. We all complimented her, although Claire was not sure if it was a true faux ami.

"How about this one?" asked Al. "You all know that Merry Christmas in Spanish is Feliz Navidad. Well, somebody thought it sounded like 'Police naughty dog.'"

That brought a good chuckle. People were laughing and having a good time with the misunderstandings of language, and every-one was eager to add his own contribution to the pot.

Vernon asked: "Do any of you know what a *mondegreen* is?" No one seemed to know. "You tell us about it," I said, encouraging him.

"A line in a song extols the magic of love, asking: 'Don't it make your brown eyes blue?' But someone heard: Donuts make your brown eyes blue. That's a mondegreen."

"Oh, that's funny. How cute. Do you know another?"

"Yes. And this is the where the name 'mondegreen' comes from. An old Scottish song goes like this: '*They hae slain the Earl of Moray and laid him on the green.*'

But this sounds very much like: 'they hae slain the Earl of Moray and Lady Mondegreen.'"

Then I jumped in with the song that Bob Hope used to sing: *Mercy dotes and dosy dotes and little lamsy divey. And kiddlesy I.V. 2, wouldn't you?*"

"It sounds like pure gibberish. But if you spell it out, they say: Mares eat oats, and does eat oats, / and little lambs eat ivy, / and kids will eat ivy too, wouldn't you?"

To Monica the song didn't click, but she didn't want to spoil the fun by  interrupting for clarifications. She gave her notebook a rest. She tuned out on the retelling of that skit in a movie of Abbot and Costello where a Chinese baseball player by the name of Hu was on the field. Vernon related the exchange.

"Who is on first?" Costello asked.

"Hu is on first," Abbott answered deadpan.

"No, I asked you, who is on first?"

"And I told you: Hu is on first."

The skit went on for several rounds. Everyone laughed heartily, but Monica only smiled politely. Then it was Claire's turn. By the laughter of the men, Monica could tell the story dealt with something spicy. It was about a man who wanted a piece of ice. But his lady friend thought he said he wanted a piece of ass.

The guests departed soon after that. Al helped take things to the kitchen, and then he went to the family room to watch the news on TV, leaving me and Monica to work on the kitchen. As we worked, we talked about the evening—the food, the company, and of course some of the stories that Monica had missed, those mares that eat oats, for one. I sang the song for her again. Monica hummed along this time. She also got squared away on the confusion of Hu and Who and was amused by the skit this time around. But the one about the piece of ice still baffled her.

"What was the business about the piece of ice?" she asked me.

"Oh, Lord, Monica, that's a little embarrassing."

"So, tell me." Insisted Monica.

"The lady friend thought he said he wanted 'a piece of ass.'"

But Monica was not amused. She didn't get it. She missed something, so I asked her: "You know the word 'ass', don't you?"

"Yes, of course. I know that."

"Then what part about it don't you get?"

"The part about the 'piece'," replied Monica.

"The piece?" I asked puzzled. "What about it? What's the problem with that?"

"Why would a man want just a 'piece' of that? What would he do with a piece? What's wrong with the whole thing?"

I really cracked up then. I could see Monica's problem. She took it too literally. I was laughing uncontrollably.

"Oh, Monica, you're so literal. You are going to kill me laughing,"

"I can't picture it," said Monica with great frustration. "I can picture a woman saying that to a man. That would make sense. That can be cut."

That sent me into more convulsions of laughter. Monica had to hold me now and prop me up. "Well then, would you cut it a la Lorena Bobbitt to get your piece?" I asked her sarcastically.

"What? Who is Lorena?"

It took me a few minutes to get sufficiently collected to tell Monica about the Lorena Bobbitt case—the woman who made the news heard around the world in 1993 when in a fit of anger she took a knife and cut off her husband's penis. Monica had not heard that story.

"Cross my heart," I began. "It took place in Manassas, Virginia. Lorena stomped out of the house with part of the penis still on her hand and drove off. Along the way she threw it out the window. But she soon realized the gravity of what she had done and called 911. A medical team retrieved it from the roadside and surgeons managed to sew it back together again. Everything ended well. She was tried but found not guilty by reason of insanity. It happens that Lorena was from Ecuador and later, on a trip back home, the president of the country, Bucaram, (something of a nut himself) decorated her with a medal of valor."

"Oh, my God, this is an Opera Buffa," said Monica, laughing.

"Yes, indeed," I said. "And there is more. Her husband also exploited the notoriety. He formed a Rock band which he called *Severed Parts*. He also made a couple movies: *John Wayne Bobbitt: Uncut* was one, but I can't remember the other. Also, he became very popular with women. Apparently, they were extremely curious about his equipment." Now it was Monica who was laughing wildly.

The next day Vernon looked for her after class and they went out for a bite. He had a present for her. She opened it nervously at the restaurant. It was a small tape recorder.

"This will help you catch the words on the run. Just push a button and you'll get the words right off the air—even as they are being spoken. You don't have to rush for your notebook. You can always transcribe them later." Vernon then showed her how it worked. She was delighted with her new toy.

"What a brilliant idea. How ideal. How nice. It is as if some time ago, I looked upon a star to make a wish, but at the time I didn't know what to ask for. So, the star said to me: 'that's all right. I will surprise you some day.' And now, here I am with her wonderful surprise before me. I love it! Thank you so much. You read my deepest wish, Vernon."

"No, I didn't. Your star whispered it to me."

She showed me her new toy later that evening, bubbling with excitement as she demonstrated how it worked, adding: "Now I can record everything you say, June, laughter and all, the good and the bad, the mares and the lambs eating oats, the man going for ice, and even Lorena's piece."

"Oh, please don't start on that again, Monica," I told her. "My ribs still hurt from laughing so hard last night."

Later that evening, when I sat alone reflecting on how much fun it had been to have Monica in our home, I wondered what would become of her. Would she come back to the States to get a master's, or maybe even a PhD? I could picture her as a professor. She would make a great one, working her little recorder to death. In the end, Monica would learn to speak English to perfection. She would see through those English traps and dance around them. She will no longer need to come to me, entrusting her ignorance to my care. My little language fledgling would have flown out of my hands, outgrowing my care. She was a Rottweiler on expressions that made no sense to her, biting into them tenaciously and tearing them apart. I'd love to remind her of those words someday. I wonder... would she *take*, or would she *get* a highfaluting piece of ice?

Monica left for Argentina some three months ago. At the airport, she remembered something. "Ah, June, I forgot to tell you... I looked up Spanish Moss and discovered that it is neither a moss nor Spanish. How is that for a misnomer?"

"Oh, Monica, we should appoint you chief of language police."

Her departure was traumatic for us, but I took comfort in the fact that we would keep in touch. We would go to Argentina, or she would return to Savannah, a city she had come to love. Of course, the big hole she left in our hearts was nothing compared to the one—of crater proportions—that she left in Vernon's heart. Vernon adored her. I believe she also loved him, but she was afraid that marriage would be a sentence of separation from her family and her country. It complicated matters considerably. She needed more time. I think they had decided to put things on hold and to play it by ear and see what the wind brought.

Things were in this sort of limbo until three weeks ago when Vernon couldn't take it anymore. He had to see her and flew to Argentina to be with her and meet her parents. I was delighted to hear that she missed him more than she had ever thought she would. They had been burning up the Internet with their daily emails. I, in the meanwhile, felt like a matchmaker with all my bets on them. I waited anxiously for every bit of news from them. I prayed and crossed my fingers tightly for Cupid to consummate their bonding.

Then, one week ago, came the news that they had been on a bus to see the Iguazu Waterfalls on the border with Brazil, a major tourist attraction. Their bus must have been driven by a maniac. It collided head-on with a truck, while it tried to pass another bus on a two-lane road and while coming to a curve. Twenty people were badly wounded and nine people were killed. Vernon and Monica were among the dead.

I denied the news vehemently. I insisted that it had to be a mistake, and I prayed for a correction from Argentina—a correction that never came. I told my husband I was going to Argentina right away. He told me he would gladly book me on the next flight, but only if I accepted the truth that their death was no mistake. I should go for closure, to support Monica's family and to attend their funeral. In time, Al's levelheadedness prevailed, and I stopped denying the truth mentally, although I could not accept it in my heart.

The pain of such grief has been unbearable. My life has been sheer torture, alternating between stupor and spasms of tears. I cannot accept an outcome so brutal, so punitive, but without cause. Why did it have to happen? Where is the justice? Why would the gods permit it? In my despair, I cursed the gods; I cursed the fates, and I started to write about my torment, flailing at the keyboard as if exploding in a torrent of words in lieu of tears. I groped for catharsis writing in rebellion and anger. But I could find no solace writing that way.

Then I realized that this narrative should not be about me, about my pain, or my suffering, but about Monica. It should not be a lament for what Monica might have been or a complaint for her stolen future. It should be, instead, a celebratory remembrance of those golden days she spent with us, a memoir of those days full of laughter over words.

Gradually, I began to cull my memory for specifics, trying to list some of the words she learned while here and trying to recall the idiomatic expressions that troubled her. She had a nose for the foibles of language and for the quirkiness of everyday expressions. I found that the recall of these lessened my sorrow. They made me smile rather than cry. This was the therapy that brought back the sunshine after a horrendous night.

True catharsis came for me when I began to write with the purpose of preserving the remembrances that were still vivid. I knew I wouldn't always remember them, and I had to work fast to recapture the vignettes, the stories, the punch lines, and the details. Some of these memories were fading already. I wished I had taken notes. I wished I could get hold of her notebook and her little recorder.

Words, I discovered, work a magic upon memory. I would see words bursting in my mind like flares on a dark night, dispersing shadows and lighting up the past. At times a metaphor would feed a word, or vice versa. I would picture Monica running after a word she fancied, like a lepidopterist after a bright yellow butter-fly. She would accommodate it gingerly in her little notebook. It was, of course, the word 'highfaluting.' Or I would see her strug-gling to catch a wayward expression that was as slippery as a piece of ice. Then I could see more and more words as they flocked be-hind her in a bright trail, like the luminescence of a comet's tail, a celestial peacock in the firmament of my mind that brought joy to my life. And I realized that we live in the minds of others through the nuggets of memory that words encapsulate—words which, in effect, immortalize us. Those words helped me write this story and share the remembrance of the unforgettable char-acter that Monica was.

# WORD METAMORPHOSIS:
# PREQUEL

---

Words change meaning at the pace of continents drifting away, sometimes taking millennia. But the word *gay* was an exception. This word changed meaning practically overnight, and all in my lifetime. I can still remember a time when it stood for cheerfulness, bubbliness. It was not the euphemism for homosexuality that it is today.

The word changed with the cultural revolution of the 1970s, when people let it all hang out and when the winds of change swept off many homosexuals out of their closets. Overnight the word changed as if it had undergone a virtual sex operation itself.

I had been writing a series of stories about words and I sensed there was a story here, but I couldn't get started. For inspiration I re-read Ovid's Metamorphosis for the umpteenth time, a book which is one of my all-time favorites and which was appropriate for my project as it is the definitive work about change in all things, in the creatures of the earth, in nature, in humanity, in everything under the sun. Ovid was a master at explaining transmogrifications. I wondered what he would have done with the change of the word *gay*.

But even Ovid would have had difficulties writing in the 21$^{st}$ Century because the world has changed so much. Our world is not the simple world of his time. We are constrained by science and rationality. In Ovid's day you could explain the world by tales and yarns, by legends and myths. But that no longer works because we are too analytical and demand quantification of facts and statistics, precisely the sort of thing that I wanted to avoid. I did not want a linguistic thesis. An ambitious graduate student could turn that into his PhD thesis and give a year-by-year chronology with tons of citations about the number of times the word was used over the airwaves, in the printed media, and so on. But this was not for me. I kept looking for an approach in the spirit of Ovid, something allegorical and mythical, but still plausible.

In Ovid's time, the mysteries of nature were explained in terms of the will and power of the gods. And the gods, except for their supernatural powers and their immortality, were like humans in every respect—especially, one might add, in their weaknesses. They were proud, selfish, jealous, capricious, lustful, busybodies, intransigent, vengeful, scheming, unfaithful, and wrathful. But when they were good, they were also kind, wise, generous, considerate, good confidants, friendly, and helpful.

Humans were often helpless bystanders caught in the middle of squabbles between the gods. One God would kill a mortal while another God—taking pity but unable to undo what the other god had wrought—would grant a compensating grace, an immortal tribute that at least would honor the memory of his hapless protégé. Thus, humans would be transmogrified in death into flowers, into fountains, trees, birds, mountains, snow, spiders, or into just about anything. The Greeks and the Romans had myths for all things under the sun.

"Ovid, you lucky rascal," I said as I perused sleepily the pages of Rolfe Humphries' translation of Metamorphosis on my desk. "You had it so easy with your gods, with your naiads and your satyrs, in that young primeval world that was yet unfettered by the strictures of rational explanations. How I envy you. I love the way you explained homosexuality with your story of *Salmacis*. So simple. So beautiful."

I must have dozed off while reading that story because I was drawn into Ovid's world. I found myself in another age, in another season, in a bucolic setting, in what appeared to be an open temple with a pergola a few yards from a small lake. It was a warm and bright summer day with a dream-like ambience that seemed so typical of Ovid, so idyllic, so pastoral. I was living the enchantment of a lazy afternoon, enjoying all its attributes, the summer heat, the smell of grass and honeysuckles, and the buzz of a bee flying nearby. As I stood up to look around beyond my immediate area, I noticed the presence of a water nymph, Salmacis, who was several yards away and headed to the pond's edge.

*Salmacis Story*. She was dancing dreamily, trying on different clothes, flinging her veils to the breeze. There was no question in my mind anymore that I was in Ovid's story. What was not clear was whether I was reading or dreaming. But it did not matter. I could have watched that nymph contentedly for hours. She was a delight to see, so young, so carefree, and so beautiful. She was running in and out of the water, splashing, and cavorting.

Then a young man came into the scene. He was handsome, around fifteen, and of godly parentage. His mother was the Goddess of Beauty, Aphrodite, no less; and his father was the God Hermes, the messenger and trouble shooter for the gods, which explains his name Hermaphroditus.

After a long trek through the woods, he came upon this lake. The sight of the water seemed heaven sent, so cool, so blue, so crystalline and irresistible. He couldn't wait to splash in for a swim. As he was taking off his gear, getting ready to plunge in, Salmacis caught sight of him, and it was love at first sight for her. She was smitten. As a beautiful young woman herself in her early twenties, she should have had beaus galore. But she lived isolated, far from the nearest village and she was lonely. She would pass her time daydreaming, thinking of love, of handsome young men, of sex and marriage. That is why the presence of this lad that afternoon was so special. Now, at last, a man, a prince, had chanced upon her world and she would grab the chance.

"Well, hello, good looking, what brings you to this neck of the woods? Haven't seen you around here before."

"Oh, hi," he said tersely. He was not of many words. "I was out hunting."

She wanted to say: "Well, you found me. I'll be your prey. You can just devour me with kisses." But she kept it to herself. For now.

"You don't look like a nature boy to me. You seem cultured and refined. In fact, I took you to be a god. You wouldn't be Cupid by any chance, would you?" She laughed after she said that.

Hermaphroditus nodded his head in denial. She came closer, smiling, flirting.

"Well, that's too bad...too bad you're not the God of Love. But then, you don't have to be Cupid to be love. To me you are just as good. Someone as handsome as you could have girls by the dozens. I bet they flock to you. I bet you've broken many hearts already. Do you have a sweetheart?" Salmacis asked him as she looped her veil around him like a lasso and pulled him to her. "Well, how about it? Are you in love with someone? Is there a lucky girl somewhere?"

He broke loose from her and ducked under her veil. She laughed and tried to play with him, but he was not amused. He went for his sack and his sandals, getting ready to depart, but she grabbed one of his sandals to make him come for it. He lunged for it and snatched it away from her. She then embraced him, imprisoning him in a loving clasp.

"If you are not engaged, then take me. I'll be yours. Let's lie down together and make love. But even if you are engaged, still take me. Your sweetheart doesn't need to know our secret. Make love to me. If you're still a virgin like me, we'll both learn together. Love will be our teacher."

Hermaphroditus broke loose and pushed her off. "Let me go! Leave me alone. I'm getting out of here."

When Salmacis realized that he was not bluffing, that he would really leave, she realized she had pushed too far. She then changed her tune. "No, no. Please don't leave. I didn't mean to be such a bother. It is I who should leave and let you enjoy the lake. Please forgive me. Let's be friends. To prove my sincerity, I will now depart and leave you alone. No hard feelings. Okay? Goodbye, dear boy. I hope we're friends when we meet again. Don't think of me bitterly. I'm sorry."

With that she left, walking dejectedly from the grassy clearing and disappearing into a grove nearby. He waited a few minutes to be sure she was really gone and then he proceeded to undress to go for his swim. But she hadn't left at all. She was hiding in the bushes, watching him, lusting after him. When she saw him fully naked, she could hardly stay calm anymore. She was feverish, overcome with desire.

He dove into the water and cavorted happily, rolling, splashing, flailing at the water and going down to the sandy bottom. She could resist no more. Off came her clothes and she ran into the water fully naked, eager, full of passion!

"You looked like you were having so much fun, I couldn't resist. Isn't it grand? Oh, this is so divine."

He smiled, agreeing about the water. She thought he had mellowed by now, so she came closer. They played around for a while, but in the end, she couldn't repress her true lascivious intent and began making overt advances. She embraced him, she kissed him, touched his body, pressed him against her, moaning: "You are mine, you're mine." He struggled, trying to disengage from her, but she had wrapped herself around him tightly like a boa, her limbs twisted around him, clutching him in an ardent grip, going for broke. She would have him or die trying. He still resisted her, and he was strong. Then in a final plea—not to him, but to the gods—she prayed: "Oh, please dear gods, let him be mine. May he never break loose from me! Keep us as one forever."

And the gods heard her prayer and granted it. Suddenly, the bodies fused into one; their faces morphed into a single composite of the two—no longer just Salmacis, just Hermaphroditus; no longer male or female, but both.

When Hermaphroditus realized what was happening, when he felt the softness of his limbs, his encroaching femaleness, he prayed to his own gods, to his parents, and begged them to put a spell upon that water so that any person bathing there would suffer the same fate. And from that time that lake holds that curse. *End of Salmacis Story.*

As soon as I finished reading (or dreaming the story), I told myself: How neat! Without getting into the tangles of genetics, or behavioral conditioning; without tendering moralistic arguments and taking sides either with those who think homosexuality is evil, or those who think it is a disease, Ovid has laid out his account of the origins of atypical sexuality in a beautiful story. That's the sort of thing I would like to do with the word *gay*: to tell a story metaphorically, out of pure allegory.

*Ovid appears.* I was still sitting in that temple in Ovid's world when I became aware of his presence. I could not see him, I could not even hear him directly, save by telepathy, as an oracle, as a friendly mentor being helpful.

"So, what's the problem?" I sensed he asked me. "You want to write about the metamorphosis of a word. So, what's stopping you?"

I responded: "The trouble is that the world has changed too much. You had your gods, and they granted wishes, and fixed things. And we don't have that in the 21st century."

"Oh, but you are wrong about that," he said. His words were so clear now. Perhaps it was my imagination, but I thought I could see him going about his chores, feeding the birds, and trimming the plants in the temple as he talked to me.

"You do have gods," he continued. "You can find them in the offices of the important institutions that run your world: The Church, Academe, Business, Philanthropic Foundations, and the Government. In the case of the Church, you should see the Pope, the head of the Anglican Church, the Dalai Lama, and the head of the Baptists, of the Lutherans, the Billy Grahams, the Jerry Falwells, and their like. In the case of government, look at the leadership, The President of the United States and his cabinet. I think you have more gods than we ever did. This is just the tip of the iceberg.

"Your world is full of gods. The trouble is that your democracy and egalitarianism get in the way of things. You think modern democracy has eliminated their might, but it hasn't. You just have hang-ups about it. You have a penchant for depersonalizing and blurring your gods. Often, rather than mention a god by name, you prefer to give his address, his digs. 'The Pentagon' you say, 'Capitol Hill, Madison Avenue, Wall Street, Hollywood, the Vatican, 10 Downing Street, the Kremlin,' and so on. I suppose this is an indirect way of recognizing the immortality of the gods, as if underscoring that its current mortal occupant may come and go, but the real god endures, the institution is forever.

"You also have lesser organizations, with lesser gods, that are service oriented, committed to a cause or to a group of people such as: the ACLU, UNESCO, the NAACP, the Sierra Club, the Red Cross, and the Humane Society, just to name a few. The point is that all your gods, big ones and lesser ones, wield a lot of power and authority, and they are constantly intervening in human affairs. At times they perform miracles; at times they are the cause of trouble. It is a mystery to me how all your gods work.

"Take Wall Street, for example. I know that Wall Street is not a person, but a street in Manhattan. But you'd never know this from hearing the commentators who refer to it as though it were a living thing, a mysterious god, one that everybody talks about, but nobody sees or understands. Millions of people follow his moods daily, hour on the hour, trying to determine what He likes and what He doesn't like; why He gets upset; why He has a good day; why He has a bad day. And when He does have a bad day, the gurus and tea leaf readers look for things to blame. Was it something another god did or said—someone like the Fed, or the Treasury? And talk about myth making! We had nothing like it. This god breeds more myth and mumbo jumbo than any ancient god. There's a lot of talk about bears and bulls. When the bulls are out, I understand, great fortunes are made; happy times are here again; the economy is as festive as Pamplona on the 7th of July. But when the bears come onto the scene everybody panics, misery is around the corner and some people jump out of buildings in despair.

"Then there is this. Just as people in my time made sacrificial offerings to the gods to keep them happy, I notice that your people put their offerings on envelopes and send them off to the gods. Contributions they call them. Then in times of need they pray to their gods and ask for help. If it is a disaster, the Red Cross is one of the first to send help. Then again, because these institutions are run by humans, they suffer from the same weaknesses that you described about my gods earlier. They are fallible and erratic. From time to time, they have been known to abuse their power and betray the trust that mortals put on them. Corruption you call it."

He finished talking. I understood Ovid's words implicitly and they rang true. I could picture scenes from the last 30 years when institutions had acted like gods for good and for bad. Pride, conceit, greed, abuse of power, dirty tricks, you name it. Washington and Hollywood kept right up with the ancient gods. All you must do is to take any shenanigan in the news and just ask yourself: what god does this behavior remind you of? The amorous antics are easy—movie stars falling in and out of love with each other prove that Cupid is alive and well, playing his pranks and working overtime in Hollywood. And there are vindictive shrewish actions in high places that have the name of Hera written all over them.

Not too long ago, for example, Ovid would have said it was Hera who was ranting and carrying on about homosexuals. But it was the "Church"—speaking like a virago, railing against homosexuals, calling their condition a vice, a damnable sin, something they did by choice, as libertines. The Church, (or Hera), went as far as to claim that AIDS was a punishment from God, implying that they deserved it. Fortunately, other gods disassociated themselves from these pronouncements and, true to the protocols of Ovid's time, while they could not undo what other gods had said or done, they could lend a hand and do what they could to be supportive. The U.S. Congress, for example, broke tradition and established a new precedent by embracing and supporting congressman Barney Frank from Massachusetts, who had come out of his closet to announce he was homosexual. In earlier years he would have had to pay extortion to keep his private life a secret. If he had been exposed, the furies would have been sent after him and he would have had no recourse but to resign his position and leave town or commit suicide. Barney Frank was the second homosexual congressman to come out of his closet while in office. The first was Gerry Studd, who was censured for improper behavior with a congressional page. Both, however, went on to be re-elected, breaking new ground. Others followed. Then, even the Pentagon, the God of War no less, took a conciliatory position on homosexuals in the military, offering an accommodation known as "Don't Ask Don't Tell." Naturally, all the muses came out to support their kindred artists. Erato, Euterpe, Thalia, Melpomene, and Terpsichore came out of their modern-day temples in Hollywood, in New York and other entertainment capitals to sponsor concerts to help with AIDS research, and to honor the homosexual artists for their achievements.

Ovid's point was well taken: the correspondence between the gods of his world and the institution of our time is, indeed, compelling. I wanted to continue communicating with Ovid but, unfortunately, the spell had been broken. The epiphany faded. I found myself in front of my computer, in the real world again, readjusting my eyes to my surroundings. While I had lost my connection with Ovid, his visit had accomplished something. I felt richer and inspired from the experience. I was still at square one on my story, but at least I wasn't drawing blanks anymore. Ovid had given me the clue and it was the gods.

# WORD METAMORPHOSIS: PART I

By the mid1960s the Vietnam War was raging, and discontent was rampant. The war was very unpopular. To add insult to injury, the Pentagon in those days met its manpower needs through the draft. Protests of all sorts flared across the land. At first it was against the war and the draft, but in time it was against the arrogance of power of our gods. Everyone had grievances in those days. In Los Angeles it was the Blacks who rose against economic repression and set Watts on fire, giving us the angry cry: "Burn, Baby, burn." The college-age youth protested the war and the draft, and burned their draft cards on the streets, chanting: "Hell no, we won't go!" Radical student groups sprouted everywhere and took over administrative offices in many universities, including Harvard.

Some student protestors got off easy, some were put in jail, but some paid dearly with their lives, as in the massacre at Kent State. This incident helped galvanize the country against the tyranny of power. More disaffected people came out of the woodwork.

Women came out into the streets to vent their anger against the machismo and male chauvinism that had held sway for centuries. They burned their bras. Whoever the goddess was, her minions were certainly visible and vocal: Gloria Steinem, Betty Friedan, and Germaine Grier among them. Even the Earth goddess rounded up her children and sent them out to protest the ravages of the environment: air pollution, acid rain, pollution of the rivers and oceans. The first Earth Day was celebrated in the early 70s. Gradually the youth changed from being the formal well-dressed, clean-cut, and well-behaved young people of the 60s to being the hairy, devil-may-care, brash and insolent bunch of the 70s that let it all hang out. Rock concerts became orgies of free love and pot smoking revelry, the most memorable of these took place in Woodstock, N.Y.

Where was Hermaphroditus during these tempestuous times? His modern reincarnation had not changed much since the time of Ovid. He was a little older now, in his mid-twenties, rather than his mid-teens. He went by the name of Herb Mercuris, which was a play of his ancient Greek and Roman names; Herb because of his father's Greek name, Hermes; and Mercuris because of his father's Roman name, Mercury.

He was enrolled at Berkeley, mainly to avoid the draft. Officially, he was pursuing a master's in art history, although he was considering changing to Architecture. He did not know. He was a dabbler at heart, trying to find himself in a world in turmoil. At this time, he was working in a firm of interior design and landscape architecture.

It was late. He was closing the elegant studio. Everyone had left for the day, except him. He was clad in the dress of the times, high heel boots, bell-bottom pants and wide leather belt. He lowered the front blinds and flipped the sign on the door to read "Closed," and then just as he closed the door, Vea, his mother, showed up from the back of the studio.

"Tah dah!" she intoned with flair, trumpeting her own entrance.

"Mother, you startled me," he said gasping. "What are you doing coming from back there? How did you get in?"

"Oh, I have my ways, you know," she said coyly. "No, really, when I came in earlier, I shushed people not to call you. You were busy. I just sat in the garden and waited. It's lovely out there."

"You look divine, as usual. Is that a Balenciaga you're wearing?"

"No. Yves St. Laurent."

"I love it. It is absolutely stunning. White becomes you. I must call Yves and congratulate him. But what's up, Mom? Do you need a quickie hair trim for tonight, or something?"

"No, I don't need anything. Nothing is up. I just came to see you because I'm still worried about you. We parted on bad terms last week, arguing as usual. We often seem to end our encounters that way these days."

"You do exaggerate. You worry too much about me, and you shouldn't."

"Sometimes I hardly recognize you," continued Vea. Her name by the way was adopted from her initials, V and A, which stood for Venus and Aphrodite. "You look as if you had the weight of the world on your soul, Herbie. And, yes, I know you are working very hard. But don't give me that. That's not it. Something troubles you. It bothers me to think that you are not happy. I wish you would let me help you, but you don't."

"Here we go again, Mother. We go through this every week. You are inventing a problem that you want me to admit to. Trouble is there is no problem; nothing is wrong, really. I'm just busy."

"All right, I think we are not going to get anywhere this time either. Very soon you are going to tell me that you have an appointment, that you must run, and we'll be left to pick up next week exactly where we left off before, in the same void. So let me get to the point that concerns me before you go running off. I wish you would confide in me more, as you used to when you were younger. I think you are not happy, and it pains me. I want to help. If that involved prying into your private life, then so be it. I do want to pry. But only so I can help you."

"Okay, what do you want to know? Would you like me to lie down in a couch and divulge my soul's secrets? Ooops, so sorry, I forgot. I don't have a couch."

"Will you please be serious?"

"Shall I just sit then? Is that okay?"

"Sitting is fine. Don't take this as a joke. I am dead serious. Please stop swatting off my questions with sarcasm. I'll come to the point and ask you, are you going out with anybody now? Do you have a love interest now? Just so you know: be it boy or girl, I don't care."

"Do I have a love interest? No, I don't. Do you?"

"Yes, I do ... your father."

"Don't make me laugh. When was the last time you saw him?"

"Four days ago. But that's beside the point. Although we are often apart because we lead very busy lives, we belong to each other, and we love each other. We've been married 26 years—that is two longer than you've been alive—and believe it or not, we have a very happy sex life, thank you. Now it's my turn to ask you a blunt question. Do you have a happy sex life?"

"Mother, I am shocked. I am stunned! I'm horrified by your question!" he said melodramatically, feigning and exaggerating true shock.

"Be shocked. Be stunned. But answer the question anyway."

"You would love to know that, wouldn't you?"

"Yes, I would. It doesn't make any difference to me who your love interest is, as long as you are happy."

"Are you hinting by any chance that I have homosexual tendencies? Whatever gave you that idea?"

"You are very effeminate, Herbie. It shows in your mannerisms, the way you talk, the way you fix your sisters' hair. Who knows? But it doesn't matter. I am not passing judgment on you. I love you as you are."

Mother and son were having one of those difficult tragi-comic dialogues in which he spoofed everything, cutting up, hiding under sarcasm, acting frivolously, reluctant to answer her questions. She was phrasing every thought in earnest, mincing no words, and wasting no time. After much evasion, he finally spoke from the heart.

"The trouble with this conversation is that you want me to either confirm or deny something I don't know. I don't know what I am, Mother. I can't say that I am homosexual because I have never actually consummated it. But neither can I say flatly that I'm not one because I think I am a latent one. What I can tell you for sure is that I am an all-around blooming cherry red virgin, with many close encounters that end up as near misses. So, there! That's the best I can do to answer your specific questions. What more do you want me to say?"

"Say no more, Herbie, my dear son. You've said enough. Thank you, thank you for what you've shared with me. I think you've been given a hard hand to play in life. But I maintain that in spite of it, you are entitled to be happy, and I am determined to help you find that happiness. That is all I want."

"What about Dad?" he asked. "How does he feel about this?"

"Have no fear. Your dad is a broad-minded man, and he loves you very dearly also. He will have no trouble accepting you as you are. He will support you and will continue to love you always. I will see him tomorrow and tell him."

"No, don't! Wait before you do that. Let me tell him. On second thought, what the hell, you tell him! I don't care. We are living in an age of rage, of 'Burn, baby, burn.' Everybody is angry and everybody is doing something about their problem—everybody except me. I am staying on the sidelines like a quiet hypocrite, pretending to be the straight young man I am not, and just going along with things as they are because I am a coward. I ought to be shouting from a mountain top: So, what if I were one? What's that to you? I ought to be leading legions through the streets demanding my right to be whatever I want to be. If I should be a homosexual, so be it. I should still be respected as a human being and recognized for my merits. I should be denouncing the discrimination and homophobic hatred homosexuals confront in all walks of life day after day. If I could change this, that would make me happy. But I know that these changes can only come by paying a hard personal price and I am afraid. It's much easier to do nothing, and I'm good at that."

Vea hugged him, saying nothing, just comforting him, being a friend and a mother at the same time. They were both a little teary eyed.

"Don't do anything rash, Herbie. Don't rush into anything. Above all, please, please, oh please, don't do drugs or seek comfort in alcohol. And one more thing, if I may be blunt. May I?"

"You, blunt, Mother? Has anyone ever stopped you?"

"Well, all right, dear. I'll be brief. If or when you should become a full-blown homosexual, be guided by these rules. Keep to your kind in all matters of love and sex. Confine your intimacy to those who are like you but be discreet and private in society. At the same time seek the friendship of straight men and women and nurture it because they are not all homophobes. People are confused about homosexuality. They just don't know and need to be educated. You must help them accept you. You are very fortunate to have the support and backing of your parents. We are powerful and can help you. Don't hesitate to seek our help. I can send the graces to help you, and I can put the muses at your disposal. There is much that we can do with our wealth and position in life to help you."

"Yes, I am aware that I am privileged, Mother; and I thank you for the support you extend me, but what about those who are not so fortunate? Think of them as if they were your sons and daughters, too. How would you help us all? And what is it that you and the muses can do for us precisely? Are you going to change the world? Are you going to eliminate the revulsion the straight world has for homosexuals? How are you going to do that? How are you going to enlighten bigots and make prejudice disappear? Do you really think the world can change through words, through culture, through your graces and your muses?"

Vea had no difficulty responding to that, she said emphatically: "Yes. That's the goal. That's what I intend to do. Your dad and I will work to minimize prejudice and create good will. You leave that to us."

"I think you are dreaming. I think that the problem is far more complex than you imagine. But let me change the subject long enough to ask you: would you like a drink?"

"Yes, I'd love a daiquiri."

Herbie went to a small kitchenette, and she followed him there. As he prepared the drink, she continued the discussion.

"Don't think I'm unaware of the complexities. I am ahead of you there. In fact, I can tell you this much. You are not ready yet. The campaign for conquering the world requires overcoming one major hurdle."

"Oh? Really? And what would that be?"

"You."

"Moi? How's that?"

"You must be ready. You must be at peace with yourself, comfortable with what you are, and I don't think you are. Are you?"

"What a question! Isn't everybody comfortable with who they are?"

"Heterosexuals are, for the most part... but I don't think homosexuals are, especially those who, like you, are latent ones and have not crossed their Rubicon."

"Whew! We are quite an oracle today, aren't we? And to think they say blonds are dumb. Here's your drink."

In this modern reincarnation of Aphrodite, Vea was a blonde. On this early evening, she was radiant, classy, and elegant like Catherine Deneuve in her forties. She sat on a chair and he across the table, facing her, as they continued their intimate tête-à-tête.

"Mother, let me tell you something. You are either so, so wrong about all this, like you're just talking and don't know what you're talking about, or you are wise beyond my comprehension. I can't tell which."

"It's the latter, of course, Silly."

"Then tell me more."

"There is no reason why you cannot be happy. Although the world is hard on you, just go about your life around the barriers, continuing your studies, developing yourself. Be patient. In time you will be able to join the fight against those barriers. For now, dedicate yourself to learning and maturing, and I don't mean just professionally. I mean personally. There are so many questions that you have yet to answer for yourself. Are you asexual? Are you bisexual? Are you transsexual? Or are you just homosexual? And if you are homosexual, what type are you? Perhaps you need guidance on these questions. Don't be afraid to look for advice, and don't be afraid to consult experts, psychiatrists, therapists or what have you. Read books. Talk to people. Become better informed."

"Thank you, thank you, Mother Teresa, for your loving concern. I agree that there is much I need to find out for myself, and much of what I need to learn is not something that you can help me with because it involves technicalities that you know nothing about. There is a limit to how far we can go talking about this sort of thing."

"Yes, I know. You're right. There's much about this issue that I don't know, or care to know. But remember, all I care about is simply that you find happiness. I see some homosexuals who accept who they are, and they go through their lives acting oh, so gay, so sybaritic, as if life was just one endless party. They exude gayness. They accept their fate; they seem to be happy in their own joyful nirvana. These are the flaming homosexuals. But then I see others that are like still water that runs deep. Who knows what maelstroms eddy underneath? These project an image of elusive normalcy under a heterosexual facade. The world is dual for them, and they function in both spheres—openly in one but clandestinely in the other—and this takes a toll. They are at war with themselves, teeter-tottering between irreconcilable worlds. I don't want you to be in this latter category. I would just as soon see you as an out-and- out flaming homosexual, but one who was outwardly happy and gay."

"... Happy and gay," he repeated, mocking her words. "Hmm, gay and joyful... Has it occurred to you that they may just be high on something? But you just said you don't want me to do that. Have you considered that deep down there may be a hellacious maelstrom in them, too? By the time they are old they are nothing but sad and withered drunken fags—if they haven't killed themselves, or someone hasn't beaten them to death."

Vea was noticeably displeased at his words. She grimaced and frowned.

"Gay and joyful ... " he continued, as if thinking of something sarcastic to riposte. "Is that the way you want me to be, gay and joyful? Okay, coming right up: I'll give it to you medium rare and gay and joyful. Would you like some French fries to go with that, too?"

"Oh, stop it! Quit being so sarcastic with me! You know perfectly well what I mean. I'm not trying to fashion your homosexual style. I just don't want you to be miserable being what you cannot change. Don't make fun of it. I'll have you any way you care to be, so long as you are happy. Is that so bad; is that so hard to understand? Why do you fight me?"

Vea was on the verge of tears, and she started to leave, but he detained her. He was truly contrite and serious now.

"I'm sorry, Mother. You're so right. I am at war with myself. I have much to sort out. And I do appreciate your concern. I do. I really do."

Mother and son hugged, both crying freely, repressing tears no longer. She stroked and patted him. They talked for a few more minutes as he had to run to class and to other commitments. But in those last few minutes he became less evasive, less sarcastic, more open, and she felt that at last she had cracked through that defensive shell of his, and past the barricades he put around himself.

# WORD METAMORPHOSIS:
# PART II

The next day Vea dropped in on Herb, her husband. He was in his New York office, a glassy aerie atop a skyscraper overlooking Manhattan, practicing his golf, putting golf balls into a little bucket. He was delighted to see her, and he kissed her effusively.

"Ah, how lovely you are, my darling. Always radiant like a sunrise, my Venus! I've missed you," he said.

"Hello, Darling. I've missed you, too."

They kissed warmly and tightly. Hermes had evolved in the 21$^{st}$ century into one of those powerful media moguls who owned and/or controlled TV networks, newspapers, magazines, movie studios, and conglomerate enterprises. He was one of those billionaires with the awesome hidden power that pulled the strings of the world stage, making and breaking powerful men, changing the economic, political and cultural scene of the globe. His influence and control extended beyond the major seats of power in the U.S. and covered the world at large. As soon as he became unclenched from the embrace, he reached for his intercom to give instructions to his secretary.

"Ms. Able, please delay my helicopter pick-up for two hours. Call the airport and tell them I will leave two hours later. Hold all my calls and take messages. I am not to be disturbed for the next two hours."

"Yes, sir. I'll get on it right away."

Then he approached Vea, saying: "I have to go to Africa. A massacre and genocide is going on there and I'll have to see what I can do to stop it, or at least negotiate a truce, and help get food to thousands of stranded people. But I am so glad you came because I don't exactly know when I'll see you again. It may be several days. So let me look at you. Let me take the memory of these two hours with me and let's make them as sweet as we can. I want your scent, your warmth, your touch, your love. I would love to take you with me, but it is too dangerous. If I were going to Paris, I would take you with me even if I had to kidnap you."

Then he began kissing her again, embracing her, fondling her, and started fumbling with her blouse as he kissed her face more and more wildly.

"Please Darling, not now. I have something important to discuss with you. Can you wait?"

"No. You wait. Let me ravish you."

"Oh H, you love nut," she said as she began unbuttoning her skirt.

Vea knew better than to press for any discussion then. It was useless. Besides, in two hours there would be time—time for problems, time for news, time for discussion, and time for love. But love had to be first, and love trumped all. They repaired half naked to his private quarters and made love that afternoon as if they had a century to spare, oblivious to all cares and concerns. An hour later, with 99 years of bliss behind them and with one hour left to spare still, they were back in his office all dressed and proper once again.

"You know, it's crazy," she began. "I flew from California for six hours to be with you for a scant two hours. We have just had one glorious hour, and it has made all those six wasted hours worthwhile. It has been truly divine. What is ironic is that later tonight when you are halfway to Africa, the paparazzi will note that I'm going out to dinner without you and the rumor mongering will begin. Are they separated? Is divorce on the horizon? Even our son has questioned the state of our marriage. Do you know what I wish for? I wish we had videotaped the whole thing this afternoon or sold ringside tickets for our happy hour. Wouldn't that shatter to pieces all their speculations? As it is, this hour will have to be kept between us as our happy little secret."

"I know, Darling. I'm sorry. I really am. There is nothing we can do about our situation for a while. Please bear with me a little longer and just think how wonderful it will be in a few more weeks when we will be together for months at a time. Anyway, you'd better tell me what you started to say before I rudely interrupted you. What was the important matter you wanted to discuss?"

"It's about our son. I wanted to expand on what I told you briefly over the phone yesterday."

Vea then related her session with him in more detail, quoting even his impertinent remarks. The latent homosexuality of their son came as no surprise. They had been expecting his admission, and they took his confession with resignation and a sense of relief. Now they would enter a new stage in their lives where everything would be in the open. Herb listened to his wife with genuine concern, giving her his undivided attention.

The modern reincarnation of Hermes was true to the character of the god in the days of Ovid. Both had reputations for being powerful and gifted, venturesome, crafty, inventive and a little naughty. Both were acclaimed for legendary feats; both were self-made men, rising from modest if not humble origins (a cave in the case of the original one), and yet both reached the pinnacles of power. Both were consummate politicians with an uncanny ability to make up with people they had angered and win them over before they became unforgiving enemies. They could patch up relations and achieve lasting reconciliations. Both had a common touch. The ancient god was considered the god of thieves, of travelers, merchants, of people who lived by their wits. His modern counterpart was liked by the working poor, by the minorities—Black Americans, Native Americans, and Hispanics. His name was often submitted as a write-in candidate for offices, which he declined. He preferred to be helpful, but in an independent way. He seldom refused service to his country and to his government. He was often drafted by presidents of both parties to chair investigatory commissions. Just as the Hermes of ancient times ran errands for the gods, his modern counterpart took assignments as a troubleshooter and as especial emissary to the trouble spots of the world, as he was doing this very afternoon. Vea knew that her son couldn't have a better person on his corner than his own father. If Herb Mercuris couldn't help, nobody could.

Vea confided her frustration. She had made promises and commitments to help, but she had no specifics. "I have promised Herbie that we would help, but frankly, between you and me, I can't seem to get a handle on any specifics of what to do. How do we change prejudice against homosexuals? How do we change revulsion into acceptance? How do we get people to accept our son as a human being, and not as a perverted freak? This is what we need help with. As a mother, I want one more thing. I want him to be well adjusted. I don't want him to suffer because of what he is. I was trying to convey this to him, and I may have expressed myself badly when I suggested that he be like those homosexuals who are at peace with themselves and act cheerful and gay. Do you know what he told me? He asked me if I wanted him 'to come medium rare and with French fries too'! I am sure he thought I was trying to fashion him according to my vision of homosexuals. Perhaps I was. But all I really want is that he'd come to terms with his circumstances and that he be happy. What can we do to lighten his burden? How can we help him feel better adjusted to his circumstance?"

"Leave it to me," said Herb. "I'll think of something. I will call him later today and express my support. I will do all I can. Count on it."

Time flew by that last hour together. Before they knew it, it was time to say goodbye. She accompanied him to the helipad and saw him take off, lingering there till he disappeared. Thanks to the marvels of modern communications, they would be apart, but in touch. Hours later he called her from the air and told her he had already talked to their son.

"How did it go?" she wanted to know.

"Herbie was very nice to me, and quite appreciative of my call. We talked at some length." The son had not been sarcastic or defensive with his father as he had been with his mother. He felt quite relieved that his coming out was behind him.

"Have no fear," he assured his wife, "our son will sort things out and he's going to be okay."

Over the next few days Herb Mercuris was swamped with work in Africa. He called Vea a few times, but his calls were brief. The problems in Africa were all too consuming and demanded his full attention. But in the quiet moments when he thought ahead, he came up with ideas. The following week he would be in Geneva for a couple of days, and then he would return to New York and finish his African mission, turning things over to the U.N. Perhaps Vea could join him in New York again while he wrapped things up there.

The first thing Vea asked Herb when they met in New York was about his campaign to help homosexuals. Unlike the gods in Ovid's day, the modern gods were powerful, but the magic was different.

"What is this business about 'word change'?" she asked him. "I could not follow your plans over the phone the other day. I didn't want to say anything while I was still unsure of what you were up to, but it sounded to me as if you were just changing the meaning of the word 'gay.' You would turn it into an euphemism for 'homosexual.' Was that it?"

"Basically, yes. That's it," admitted Herb. "You wanted our son to be happy and gay, didn't you? Well, let's start by calling him 'gay.'"

"Is that going to make him happy, just like that?"

"In part, yes! To some extent you are what you are called—especially if it is flattering. You find yourself trying to live up to what you're called. You'll see. I've already started the ball rolling. You are soon going to see a whirlwind sweep across the world. It will bring with it a refreshing air that is going to change the way we think of homosexuals."

Vea was skeptical about the scheme, and yet she knew that Herb usually knew what he was doing, and he hardly ever failed at anything he tried. He was not an idle visionary, but a doer with a long list of accomplishments to his credit. That very afternoon he began putting his plan into action. He dictated memos to Ms. Able, making calls, setting up things, spinning his web. There would be parties and social functions with great exposure in the press. Herb himself would start using the word "gay" subtly, with a catchy double-entendre that would amuse people and make them take note. At times he would use it as a synonym for homosexual; at times he would use it as a synonym for bon vivant, and at times you could take "gay" to mean both: homosexual and bon vivant, as thought they were inseparable traits. Herb made sure, of course, that his remarks were quoted on all the media he controlled.

There have always been successful, well-off avant-garde intellectual homosexuals—people such as Gore Vidal, Tennessee Williams, Truman Capote, and James Baldwin—who were open about their homosexuality and who could get away with it. But this was still not the norm in the early 70s. Many actors of stage and screen, professionals, and politicians were still well-absconded in the heterosexual world, hiding under facades, pretending to be straight—some masquerading as married paterfamilias. Herb called on the famous and notorious homosexuals and enlisted them to his campaign, giving them exposure in his magazines, in his newspapers and television outlets, injecting the word 'gay' in its ambiguous sense whenever and wherever it fit. That word, which was already a buzzword in social circles, was beginning to catch on in the airwaves, especially in the talk shows of Johnny Carson, Joey Bishop, Dick Cavett, Mike Douglas, and Merv Griffin. He did not miss a one.

Vea, who saw him in action, who heard him plant the word, and who knew what he was up to, kept her reservations to herself. She was still unconvinced and unclear about the scheme but had never had the opportunity to have Herb explain it to her in detail until one night when there was a lull in his frenetic pace, and they were at home alone.

"Darling, I still don't get it. I must be missing something. Even if the word 'gay' could do magic and turn homosexuals into gay persons overnight, how does that improve the climate of the world around them; how does that lessen the hostility they face?"

"You look so beautiful when you are bothered by something...did you know that? I love that helpless countenance, that pleading and entreating look as you make your request. It turns me on. I could just..."

"Oh no! Not this time—I'm not making any concessions. Just hold your horses. We have all night. There will be nothing until I am fully clear about all aspects of your scheme. You explain. Start talking," she said firmly.

"Gee, okay, then in that case I'll talk as fast as I can," he said. "I see by your question that I may have overemphasized the bubbly effects of the word 'gay' at the expense of other considerations. It's not so much that the word 'gay' will make homosexuals feel cheerful as such. What it will do is unburden them from being forever branded by the word 'homosexual,' which is too long, too unwieldy, and it is loaded with jagged edges. It will lift the cross of that word for them and this is all for the good. This word has got to go. If the prefix 'homo' doesn't get you, then its suffix 'sexual' will rip you open. This word is too clinical. It calls attention to with-whom and what it is they do, and it is like a crown of thorns that homosexuals are forced to wear. Remember, people are basically puritanical. They don't like to talk about sex. Sex is something that only perverts enjoy and relish, the rest of mankind, supposedly, brooks it only for the purpose of procreation. The word 'sexual' opens something scabrous and problematic with which people are not comfortable. The Church, for example, didn't want to deal with the subject; it went to great lengths to have Jesus die a virgin, to insist on celibacy for the priests, to ban women from being priests. When it came to the birth of Jesus, it couldn't see sex even for procreation, so, it had to invent Immaculate Conception to have procreation without sex. Remember also that sex outside of marriage is fornication, and fornication is a sin. In sum, the word 'sexual' carries a lot of unpleasant baggage. It is strident and jarring. But homosexuals can't avoid it. They have been unfairly stuck with it. By contrast, the technical appellation for the rest of us is 'heterosexual,' but nobody calls us that. Our heterosexuality is a technicality that is left out of our moniker. Why should they be stuck with the clinical term? The word "homosexual" has its place in medical books, in technical language, but not in common use. And yet, that's all the homosexuals have. It's either that or 'queer,' or 'faggot,' or other pejorative words. So, the first part of my scheme is to come up with an alternative to that obnoxious word.

"But there is more," he continued. "Don't forget, homosexuals are not the only ones involved in this verbal web. The heterosexuals are also entangled in it. They, too, may not like using the clinical word. It would be much easier for them if there was a word, a euphemism that could extricate them gracefully out of the prickly subject. Euphemisms are the lubricants of language that ease communication among people. And the word 'gay' fits the bill beautifully. It is long overdue. The world has thirsted for this word for thousands of years. I'm convinced that it will help people on both sides to deal with the issue. Once people start using the kinder gentler word, it will open avenues to be more conciliatory, more empathetic and more human to them. Just listen to the difference. Note how bland it is to say it and to hear it. Can you see my point? Are you clear now?"

Vea not only saw the plan and logic of his scheme, but she also believed that he could pull it off. She knew he could turn dreams into reality. He inspired her. She approached him languorously, puckering her lips as if she were going to devour him with kisses. "Yes, yes, oh, yes, you smart heterosexual beast. I do understand now. You are so sexy when you lecture. Did you know that? Hmmmm!"

That night they kissed; they embraced; they cavorted and made love, feeling unburned by all problems, leaving the world behind.

As to the word 'gay,' it soon became history. Homosexuals took to it as if it were bright and florid apparel. They put it on. It fit well and they made it their uniform. The rest of the world also took to it readily because it was easy and free of acrimony and offense. The word not only opened doors, but it turned doors into automatic sliding doors.

Once Herb set his plan in motion things fell in place like clockwork. It was like his previous successes: as when he hid the cows that he had stolen from Apollo. As when he put Argos to sleep. Argos being the giant watchman that Hera had created and supplied with a thousand eyes, so nothing would get past him as he watched over Io, the young mistress of her husband whom Hera had vengefully converted into a cow. But Argos was no match for wily Hermes. Hermes freed Io by putting Argos to sleep. How did he accomplish this? He told Argos boring stories. Every story was so boring that it put one of Argos' eyes to sleep. Story by story, and eye by eye, he put all his thousand eyes to sleep, making Argos the first (and perhaps the only being, ever) to die from sheer boredom.

The tricks and schemes that Hermes employed were devilishly effective. True to form, he was putting his astuteness to work on the word "gay." His old magic went to work swiftly, pervasively, and unerringly on the dissemination of the word. As Ovid might have put it: It was as if Zephyrus whispered it to the gale, to the East wind and to the West wind. They carried its echo on the currents of the jet stream and relayed it to the trade winds that wrapped around the earth.

Like a fecund seed the word took root wherever it landed, requiring no translation because people everywhere, on virtually all the continents of the earth, took to it warmly and adopted it into their languages.

The actual mechanism of transference that the modern Hermes used was different than that in Ovid's time; it used the wireless transmission and the complex telemetry that bounced the word from satellites and diffused its new usage electronically through the mesh of our modern communication networks and the media grapevine. But it worked. The word 'gay' largely supplanted the word 'homosexual,' removing an impediment to civil discourse. The sun shone through as if emerging from an eclipse, or from behind a dark cloud, dispelling the apprehensions of inclement language. The word 'gay' went on to break all the records for universal usage and ubiquitous recognition. You now find it in many of the languages spoken throughout the world, from Tagalog to Afrikaans, to all the romance languages. There's hardly a place on earth where its meaning is not known. Gay has become the euphemism of choice around the world. Its acceptance is truly vast. It is truly a World Word. Everybody loves to use it in lieu of its alternative. It is a word that needed to be created—whether by human invention, or by the munificence of a god, or both. And so, it was.

# ACKNOWLEDGEMENTS

Grateful acknowledgement is made to INDIANA UNIVERSITY PRESS for permission to quote from Ovid's Metamorphoses translation by Rolf Humphries, Bloomington, IN: Indiana UP, 1955.

# BIOGRAPHY

Edward L. Alban (Eddie to friends and colleagues) was born in Ecuador in 1938. He settled in Savannah, Georgia in 1952, and married his wife JoAnn in 1965. They raised two children together. A professor of Economics, he has taught at Auburn University, SUNY Potsdam, Armstrong State University and Savannah State University. He retired in 2000 and has been writing poetry and fiction ever since.

In his retirement, he and JoAnn have traveled throughout Europe and South America, pursuing his new avocation for languages and literature and publishing poetry, fiction and nonfiction.